THE BIG BEAST SALE

BY THE BEASTLY BOYS

ILLUSTRATED BY JONNY DUDDLE

SIMON AND SCHUSTER

SIMON AND SCHUSTER
First published in Great Britain in 2011 by Simon and Schuster UK Ltd
A CBS COMPANY
This paperback edition published in 2012

1 3 5 7 9 10 8 6 4 2

Simon & Schuster UK Ltd
1st Floor,
222 Gray's Inn Road,
London WC1X 8HB.

www.simonandschuster.co.uk

Simon & Schuster Australia, Sydney
Simon & Schuster India, New Delhi

A CIP catalogue copy for this book is available from the British Library.

ISBN: 978-0-85707-523-9

This book is a work of fiction. Names, characters, places and incidents
are either a product of the author's imagination or are used fictitiously.
Any resemblance to actual people, living or dead,
events or locales, is entirely coincidental.

Printed and bound by CPI Group (UK) Ltd, Croydon CR0 4YY

TONIGHT,
LOOK UP AT THE MOON.
LOOK AT IT CLOSELY.
STARE AT IT.
NOW ASK YOURSELF:
AM I FEELING
BRAVE?

CHAPTER ONE

One cold winter's evening, a man in a long fur coat strode along the snowy streets of Capitol City. He turned up his collar to hide his face, his eyes darting left and right at people and cars passing by. At the corner of a dingy side street he glanced behind him and called, 'Blud, Bone, get a move on.'

Two men were following: a small man, Blud, who was dabbing his nose with a red rag, and a big man, Bone, whose beard was frosted with icicles.

'But I'm fr–freezing c–c–cold, B–b–baron Marackai,' the big man Bone said, trudging nearer.

1

'And I've got the sniffs, Sir,' the small man Blud added.

Baron Marackai glared at them both impatiently. 'Stop complaining, you wimps. There's business to attend to. *This* is where my plan begins.' He brushed the snow from a sign at the entrance to the side street, revealing the words **WILDCAT ALLEY**.

Blud skittered to the Baron's side. 'What plan, Sir?'

'My revenge against the RSPCB, of course! This time I shall finish them once and for all. Now, follow me.' Baron Marackai glanced up and down the street, checking he wasn't being watched, then strode into Wildcat Alley, his serpent-skin boots crunching on its snowy cobbles.

Wildcat Alley seemed deserted. Along its length, on either side, stood shops that looked like they hadn't sold a thing in years: a shabby hat shop, a crusty pie shop, a dusty wig shop, a run-down chemist, a greasy café, a scruffy shoe shop, and shops selling tatty furniture, clothes and ornaments. It was the end of the day and all the shops' signs were now turned to CLOSED.

The Baron stopped at the only shop with its light still on. It was a butcher's and its windows were steamy. He peered in at a crowd of people gathered inside. 'Good. They're here, just as I requested. Keep watch, you two. Don't let anyone else in.'

'Yes, Sir. Whatever you say, Sir,' Blud and Bone replied.

The Baron pushed open the door to the butcher's shop and a bell tinkled, causing the people inside to turn and look at him as he entered. The Baron forced his twisted face into a smile. 'Shopkeepers of Wildcat Alley, how wonderful to see you all,' he said, closing the door behind him and shaking the snow from his fur coat.

'It's been a long time, Baron,' Sam Enema, the butcher, replied. 'What brings you to Capitol City?'

'And why ask for a secret meeting?' Henry

Foxton, the owner of Wildcat Alley's hat shop, added.

'Because I have exciting news for you all,' Baron Marackai replied, surveying the gathering of shopkeepers. 'I know the whereabouts of some very rare beasts! Beasts from which you could make the finest goods to sell in your shops. And they're right here in this city.'

'*Beasts! Here in Capitol City?*' Jemima Fatchuck the pie seller exclaimed.

The Baron nodded. 'And I know how to get my hands on them.'

A ripple of excitement spread among the shopkeepers.

'What kinds of beasts, Baron?' Tony Malone the furniture seller asked.

'All kinds: an impossipus… a slurper…' The Baron edged a step closer, his eyes widening. 'And for a higher price, I could even get you metamorphs too.'

'*Metamorphs!*' The crowd gasped.

'Oh yes, metamorphs: the most elusive

of beasts,' the Baron replied, grinning.

Henry Foxton the hat seller raised a trembling hand. 'But times have changed, Baron Marackai – aren't you forgetting the RSPCB? If they catch us selling beast goods here these days they'll have us arrested,' he said nervously.

But the Baron merely laughed. 'Have faith, Mr Foxton. I have a plan, and by the time I'm through with it *everyone* in this city will despise beasts just as much as we do. People will be queuing up to buy beast goods at your shops and the RSPCB won't be able to do a thing about it!' He stepped among the shopkeepers gesticulating wildly. 'Fellow beast-haters, these shops used to sell the finest beast goods available: troll sausages, yeti-fur jumpers, fairy jam. It's disgraceful that you're now reduced to trying to scrape a living selling common tat. Your ancestors would be ashamed! Do as I say, and Wildcat Alley will be beastly again!'

The shopkeepers conferred, chatting

enthusiastically, excited by the thought of reviving their businesses.

'We can chop 'em!' Sam Enema the butcher said.

'And boil 'em!' Jemima Fatchuck the pie seller said.

'And stitch 'em!' Bettina Scrag the bag seller said.

'Yes, that's more like it!' the Baron told them. 'It's time to prepare your beast mincers, exterminators and extractors; oil your skinning machines and pulpers, get out your beast recipes and cooking pots.' He raised his right hand and wiggled a fleshy stump where his little finger was missing. 'Now, repeat after me: "DEATH TO THE RSPCB!"'

The shopkeepers raised their right hands and folded down their little fingers. 'Death to the RSPCB!' they repeated. All except Mr Foxton, who was putting on his hat and edging towards the door.

The Baron strode over to him and placed his hand on the hat seller's shoulder. 'Now,

Mr Foxton. You aren't chickening out, are you? Still worried about the RSPCB? Come with me and I will show you a beast that I'm sure will change your mind...'

CHAPTER TWO

The following morning, as dawn broke at the headquarters of the Royal Society for the Prevention of Cruelty to Beasts, Ulf could be found sitting on the snowy roof of his den. He had a book laid open on his lap, and was glancing at it, listening to the sounds of beasts waking across the beast park. From the meat-eater's enclosure he heard the howls of hellhounds, from the Great Grazing Grounds the bellow of a spined armourpod, and from the snowy peak of Sunset Mountain the whistling of mimis. He heard the bulltoxic grunting in the paddock, a magnaturtle warbling in the freshwater lake, griffins cawing in the aviary, and the roar of a yeti from the biodomes. All around the rescue centre, beasts were waking to the day.

A sparkle whizzed towards him from the Dark Forest. It was his best friend Tiana, a woodland fairy. 'Good morning, Ulf. What are you doing up so early?' she asked.

'I'm learning about beast calls from the Professor's book,' Ulf replied. 'It lists more than five hundred different varieties.'

The fairy shook a snowflake from her crocus petal dress then perched on the book to see. It was *The Book of Beasts*, a notebook containing secrets about every kind of beast imaginable. It had once belonged to Professor Farraway, the world's first cryptozoologist, an expert on rare and endangered beasts.

'Aren't you cold, Ulf?' Tiana asked.

Ulf had on only a T-shirt and jeans, and his bare hairy feet were nestled in the snow. 'I'm fine,' he said. He didn't feel the cold like a normal boy – Ulf was beast blood, a young werewolf who had been brought to the beast

rescue centre more than ten years ago when he was just one month old. 'I'm waiting for the Professor,' he said, glancing across the beast park to a figure on a quad bike. 'He's on his way back from feeding the flaming squid in the lagoon. He's promised to teach me how to hatch griffins' eggs.'

At that moment Ulf heard a 'BLURGH!' from behind him and glanced round, recognising the sound. 'Druce, is that you?'

There came a gurgled giggle from behind his den.

'Druce, we know you're there,' Tiana said, darting across the den roof and peeping over its edge.

The ugly face of Druce the gargoyle peered up and his long yellow tongue flicked out, soaking the fairy in spit.

'Eurgh!' Tiana shrieked. 'Druce, stop that!'

'Blurgh!' The gargoyle blew a raspberry at her then scampered away, clambering up a drainpipe on to Farraway Hall, a large country house at the edge of the beast park. Tiana chased after him.

Ulf smiled, watching them play: the fairy trying to blast the gargoyle with her sparkles, and Druce flicking spit at her with his long yellow tongue.

Ulf turned, hearing the *pop pop* of Professor Farraway's quad bike approaching. The Professor was steering the bike with one hand, talking into a walkie-talkie in the other.

Ulf called to him, 'Professor, can we hatch the griffins' eggs now?'

'Sorry, Ulf, I've got to see Dr Fielding in her office straightaway,' the Professor called back. 'Something's come up.' And he turned into the yard, heading to the house. *That's odd*, Ulf thought. *It's unlike the Professor not to keep a promise.*

Ulf had spent a great deal of time with Professor Farraway lately, learning about beasts as part of his training to become an RSPCB agent. The Professor was quite a character — more than a hundred years ago he'd founded the RSPCB rescue centre himself. And for the last fifty years he'd even been a beast too: a ghost that had haunted Farraway Hall. Recently, Ulf had sprayed his ghost with phoenix tears, a chemical that could rejuvenate the dead, and now the Professor was enjoying his second human existence.

Ulf slipped *The Book of Beasts* into his shoulder bag, then climbed down from the roof of his den and ran up the side of the paddock to the house, curious to find out what was going on. He was about to head indoors when Orson the giant stepped round from the forecourt, pushing the RSPCB truck.

'Morning, Ulf,' the giant said. 'You might not want to go in there just now. Dr Fielding's in a bit of a fluster.'

Orson was the big beast handler who helped out with the heavy jobs, and Dr Fielding was the RSPCB vet in charge at the centre.

'In a fluster about what?' Ulf asked.

'There's been some kind of trouble,' Orson replied, pushing the truck across the yard like a wheelbarrow. 'She's asked me to get the truck ready for a mission.' The giant reached into the kit room and pulled out a beast harness.

'What kind of mission?'

The giant shrugged. 'She didn't mention.'

Ulf glanced to Dr Fielding's office window and saw her talking with Professor Farraway inside. Now he was *even more* curious to know what was going on. As Orson loaded the beast harness on to the truck's open back, Ulf called up to Tiana on the rooftop. 'Psst, Tiana, stop chasing Druce and come with me,' he said. 'Something's up.'

The fairy flew down and together they slipped into the house and listened at the door of Dr Fielding's office as she spoke with the Professor inside.

'It's terrible, Professor, it's all over the front page of this morning's newspaper,' Ulf heard Dr Fielding say.

'I'm as shocked as you are,' Professor Farraway replied.

There came the sound of pages being turned.

'What's going on in there?' Tiana whispered.

'I don't know,' Ulf said. He tried peeping through the keyhole, but then footsteps sounded and the door opened.

'I *thought* I heard whispering. What are you two up to?' Dr Fielding said, catching them.

'We were just—'

'Eavesdropping is the word, I think you'll find,' Dr Fielding said. She smiled. 'Well, I suppose you'd better come in and read about it for yourselves.' She pointed to a copy of the *City Gazette* newspaper on her desk. Ulf stepped over and read its front page:

BEAST ATTACK IN CAPITOL CITY!
Report by Dolores Larkin

Citizens today are waking to the realisation that there is a monster in our city – a tentacled beast in City Park lake. Late last night it claimed its first victim. Passers-by saw an as-yet-unidentified man being dragged under the water and eaten alive. The *City Gazette* has contacted the RSPCB for comment, and it appears that the RSPCB was aware of this beast all along...

'There's a beast in the city? In the park lake?' Ulf asked, surprised.

'Yes, an impossipus,' Dr Fielding replied. 'But we hadn't deemed it to be dangerous. It's been living there secretly for years.'

Professor Farraway paced anxiously. 'Why would it suddenly attack?' he muttered. 'It's a good-natured beast. And I've never known an impossipus to eat a human.'

'We're going to have to get it out of the city, and fast,' Dr Fielding explained. 'Not only has a member of the public died, but the reputation of the RSPCB is now on the line too. I've had the reporter from the *City Gazette* on the phone asking why the public hadn't been told about the beast, and now even Major Brigstock of the army too.'

'The army?' Ulf asked.

'Yes. The public are demanding protection. If we don't get that impossipus out of the city at once, the army will open fire on it.'

Ulf gulped anxiously.

'The truck's ready to go,' Orson called from outside. Ulf saw the giant's big face looking in through the office window.

Dr Fielding gave Orson a thumb's-up then turned to Professor Farraway. 'Professor, if you can drive to the city and get the beast harnessed, I'll bring the helicopter to airlift it out.'

Professor Farraway nodded. 'I'll leave right away,' he said.

'Can I come?' Ulf asked.

Dr Fielding frowned. 'Hmm, that might not be a good idea, Ulf.'

'But I could help. I'm training to be an RSPCB agent, remember.'

Dr Fielding knelt to face him. '**Ulf, there's more to this than you realise. There are other beasts in the city too, beasts that the public are still unaware of and who absolutely** depend on secrecy to live there. You turning up might not be a good idea.'

'Why not?' Ulf asked.

'Because they're metamorphs, Ulf – beasts that look human but can transform. Beasts like you.'

'Like werewolves?'

'Similar, yes: werecats, owl-men, spidrax, froglanoids; and they live among the public without anyone knowing. If a werewolf turned up now, people might start asking more questions, and the metamorphs' cover could be blown.'

Ulf thought for a moment. 'But if I don't tell anyone I'm a werewolf then no one need know.'

Dr Fielding sighed, frustrated by Ulf's stubbornness. 'Well, okay, Ulf. If you promise not to tell anyone you're a werewolf, and to stay with the Professor at all times, I'll let you go.'

'I promise!' Ulf said. 'Brilliant! Thank you, Doctor Fielding.'

Tiana zipped to Dr Fielding's shoulder.

'What about me? Can I go too?'

'You'd better fly with me in the helicopter,' Dr Fielding replied.

The fairy smiled. 'That suits me. I love flying!'

'Then I'll see you there, Tiana,' Ulf told her, and he raced out of the office. 'Hurry, Professor — Capitol City, here we come!'

CHAPTER THREE

Ulf peered excitedly through the windscreen of the RSPCB truck as its wipers swished back and forth against the falling snow. The truck was speeding along the busiest road he'd ever seen, roaring down the middle of three lanes of vehicles: cars, lorries, coaches and motorbikes, all heading to a large metropolis in the distance with tall buildings rising from it.

'Capitol City's straight ahead,' the Professor said. He'd been driving for an hour, his foot pressed to the accelerator most of the way. 'It looks much bigger than when I last visited. I used to travel here many years ago to check on the beasts. I must say it's more fun travelling with you than the last passenger I had.'

'Who was that, Professor?' Ulf asked.

'Marackai,' the Professor replied gravely. 'When he was just a young boy, of course.'

Marackai. Ulf hated hearing that name. Marackai was Professor Farraway's son, but he wasn't anything like his father – he hated beasts and hunted them.

'I could never leave Marackai back at Farraway Hall or he'd poke and prod the beasts there in my absence,' the Professor explained. 'He was a very cruel little boy.'

Ulf frowned. Marackai was a grown man now, and five times in recent months he had tried to destroy the RSPCB and take back Farraway Hall for himself. Each time Ulf had defeated him, the last time with the help of an army of zombies. Since then the RSPCB's network of spotters had been placed on high alert, but there had been no sighting of the wicked beast hunter for weeks.

To change the subject, Ulf opened his

shoulder bag and took out *The Book of Beasts*. 'Professor, will you tell me about the impossipus?' he asked. 'How come it lives in the city?'

'She was just a baby when I used to visit her,' the Professor explained, speeding past a lorry. 'I named her Tomiko. It means "lucky" – she was an escapee from the old beast trade.'

'What do you mean, Professor?'

'Many years ago, Capitol City was the centre for the trade in beasts, Ulf. It was a horrible business: beast furs, beast skins, hats made from beasts, jams made from beasts – you name it, someone would be selling it. But when I began the RSPCB, the beast trade was made illegal.'

The truck swerved right as the Professor overtook a coach full of humans. 'Tomiko the impossipus escaped from a shop that was planning to turn her into beast goods. She found a new home for herself in the lake at City Park, and she's lived there ever since, unknown to humans.'

Until now, Ulf thought, as they turned off the motorway. They crossed a huge bridge over a river into the city, then drove along a snowy street through slow-moving traffic, past houses, shops and offices. Hundreds of humans were hurrying along the pavements in warm winter coats, swaddled in scarves, hats and gloves. A newspaper seller on the street corner called out, 'Read all about it – Beast attack in Capitol City!'

Ulf glanced back to *The Book of Beasts,* flicking to a page marked Impossipus:

An Impossipus is a rare freshwater relation of the jellyhead sea monster. It gets its name from the curious fact that it has more tentacles than are possible to count, the structure of each resembling the branches of a tree, with primary trunk tentacles extending from its spherical body and further smaller tentacles coming off in turn.

The Professor beeped the truck's horn, and Ulf glanced up, seeing a crowd of humans ahead, streaming through open metal gates with the words CITY PARK written at their top. The crowd parted, and the Professor drove slowly through. As the truck passed by, some people spotted the letters RSPCB on the vehicle's side and started shouting, 'Why didn't the RSPCB tell us about this dangerous monster?' ... 'We've a right to be safe!'

A gloved fist banged on Ulf's window, and a man yelled, 'Hey, protect humans, not beasts!'

Furious faces peered in the truck's windows as the crowd jostled on either side.

'I don't like the look of this, Professor,' Ulf said. 'Everyone's angry.'

Professor Farraway edged the truck forward through the crowd. 'They're just scared because of the attack, Ulf. Sometimes when humans get scared, they get angry too.'

The crowd was growing larger all the time, hundreds of humans pushing into the snowy park. A woman jogged alongside the Professor's window, holding a voice recorder to the glass. 'Dolores Larkin, *City Gazette*,' she said. 'Will the beast be exterminated?'

Ulf remembered her name from the article in the newspaper in Dr Fielding's office that morning.

Professor Farraway beeped the truck's horn and drove through the crowd, leaving the reporter behind. 'We must stay focused on the job in hand, Ulf,' he said, ignoring her.

They arrived at a huge lake in the centre of the snowy park. It was surrounded by a line of red-and-white tape to keep the crowd back. Soldiers were standing beyond the tape, some with rifles aimed at the water. As the RSPCB truck arrived, a soldier lifted the tape and waved it through.

The Professor parked up and switched off the truck's engine. 'Ready to get this impossipus then, Ulf?' he asked.

'Ready,' Ulf said.

They both got out and hurried to the back of the truck to unload the beast harness. Ulf was lifting it on to the Professor's shoulders when an army officer came over.

'Professor Farraway, I was told to expect you,' the officer said. 'I'm Major Brigstock.'

'So what precisely happened here, Major?' Professor Farraway asked.

'The monster is said to have burst up from under the ice and gobbled a man whole. There's not a scrap of him left.'

Ulf could see great chunks of smashed ice floating on the water as if there had been a struggle, but the lake looked eerily calm now.

'We've been keeping watch all morning,' Major Brigstock continued. 'But it hasn't shown itself since the attack.'

'We'll take over from here,' Professor Farraway told the Major. He glanced at a line of rowing boats by the water's edge. 'We'll need to borrow a couple of those.'

'Help yourselves,' Major Brigstock replied. 'But I can't be held responsible if you're attacked too.'

Professor Farraway nodded. 'Let's go, Ulf.' And he strode towards the boats. 'We'll take one each so we can spread out the harness. An adult impossipus can have a tentacle span of over fifteen metres.'

Ulf helped the Professor into one of the boats then carefully stepped into another and sat down. He took hold of its oars and was about to start rowing after the Professor when a woman came running from the crowd calling, 'Wait for me!'

It was Dolores Larkin again, the reporter from the *City Gazette*. She flashed an ID card at Major Brigstock and stepped to the water's edge. 'May I join you?' she asked.

Professor Farraway called out, 'I'm terribly sorry, but we've no room for passengers.'

'It's important that the public know what's happening,' the woman said, climbing into the back of Ulf's boat.

'Erm, I don't think you should do that,' Ulf told her. 'It could be dangerous out there.'

The woman wobbled as the boat rocked. 'Oh, I'm not averse to a bit of danger,' she said, sitting down.

Professor Farraway looked cross. 'Miss Larkin, I must insist that you—'

'And I must insist too,' the reporter called. 'The public deserve to know exactly what's going on here, and it's my duty to report it.'

The Professor raised his eyebrows. 'Well, Ulf, if you don't mind,' he said.

Ulf shrugged. The reporter seemed determined to stay. 'I don't mind, Professor. Let's just find this beast.' And he rowed out after the Professor, heading across the lake. Somewhere beneath its icy surface, the impossipus was lurking.

BEASTLY BUSINESS

CHAPTER FOUR

Meanwhile, six blocks away, Blud and Bone stood shivering outside the padlocked entrance of a disused underground-train station.

'This is the place,' Blud said. 'Smash it open, then.'

'Why do I always have to do the heavy work?' Bone complained, taking a large holdall from his shoulder.

'Because the Baron said so. You know the plan. Now hurry up.'

From the holdall Bone pulled out a sledgehammer and swung it at the train station's entrance, smashing the padlock.

Blud pulled open the gate and shone a torch

down a flight of steps inside. 'Follow me. Rumbold's down here somewhere,' he said.

'Rumbold?' Bone asked. 'Who's Rumbold?'

'The Baron said that's its name.'

By torchlight, they walked down on to the station's deserted platform then climbed down on to the old train track, continuing into a tunnel.

Blud stopped and pressed his ear to the tunnel wall. 'Now make another hole here, Bone. It'll lead us to the sewer where Rumbold's supposed to live.'

The sound of running water could be heard coming from the other side of the wall.

Bone bashed the wall with the sledgehammer, opening up a hole, and a stinking smell seeped through.

'Phwoargh!' both men said.

Bone smashed the sledgehammer at the wall again and again, making the hole large, then they stepped through into a long dark sewer full of dirty water. They gasped, sinking waist-deep. It was disgusting!

From inside his jacket, Blud pulled out two strings of sausages.

'Oh goodie, you brought lunch,' Bone said.

'These aren't lunch. They're bait!' Blud replied. He pushed through the foul-smelling water, shining his torch up and down the sewer. 'Time for din-dins, Rumbold,' he called, his voice echoing. 'Come and get it!'

Blud and Bone twirled the strings of sausages, wafting their smell along the sewer, and a belching sound echoed in the darkness ahead. A large, blubbery beast came sloshing towards them.

'It's 'orrible!' Bone said, the torchlight shining on it.

It was indeed: an enormous, slimy beast that looked like a giant slug.

'That's it, Rumbold, follow the smell,' Blud called, still twirling the sausages.

Blud and Bone turned and quickly clambered back through the hole to the underground station, coaxing the beast from the sewer. It wobbled after them, its huge

gummy mouth opening like a dribbling cave.

'Okay, brace yourself,' Blud said. 'Now comes the scary part.'

Still clutching the sausages, the two men hugged one another, whimpering with fear.

'There's a good beast. Be gentle. Please be gentle.'

CHAPTER FIVE

Back in City Park, Ulf rowed his boat between the floating chunks of ice, following Professor Farraway to the middle of the lake. The crowd on the shore had hushed and were watching intently. All Ulf could hear was the creak of the oars in the rowlocks, and the plop of the blades in the water.

Dolores Larkin took a voice recorder from her pocket and whispered into it, 'RSPCB agents are bravely going to retrieve the City Park beast – or the Underwater Gripper as citizens are now calling it.'

Ulf gulped nervously, pulling on the oars. He peered into the icy water, looking for signs of the impossipus. 'Professor,' he called. 'How are we going to get the beast to the surface?'

'I want you to copy me, Ulf,' Professor Farraway replied, lifting his oars from the water and letting his boat drift. 'Dip your hands over the side of your boat and gently flap them in the water, like this.' The Professor leaned from his boat, plunging his hands into the icy lake. 'Try to imitate the paddling feet of a duck.'

'A duck?' Ulf asked.

'Yes, there's nothing Tomiko likes to eat more than a juicy duck, and they're scarce at this time of year. If Tomiko's down there, she'll sense the vibrations and come looking for a meal.'

Ulf pulled his oars into the boat then dipped his hands into the cold water, flapping them to imitate the movement of a duck's feet. He tried not to think of the beast's tentacles shooting up from below and grabbing him.

Dolores Larkin peered over his shoulder. 'Do you think that's why the impossipus ate the man?' she asked.

'Pardon?' Ulf asked confused.

'Because it ran out of ducks?'

'Maybe, Miss Larkin, though the Professor says he's never known an impossipus to eat a human before.'

'Is that gentleman in the other boat a Professor?' she asked, holding the voice recorder out to Ulf.

'Yes, his name's Professor Farraway. He's an expert on beasts. And I'm Ulf.'

'Aren't you cold, Ulf? No coat? No hat? No gloves?'

'It's okay, I'm a—' Ulf nearly told the reporter that he was a werewolf, but stopped himself just in time, remembering what he'd promised Dr Fielding. 'I'm… err … warm from rowing,' he said quickly. He looked into the water, seeing a stream of bubbles rising from the depths and popping as they reached the surface. 'Professor, something's happening over here,' he called. 'There are bubbles.'

'That'll be Tomiko, Ulf,' the Professor replied. 'She's coming up!'

Suddenly Ulf saw a man's hat bob up too.

'Oh look, how strange: a hat,' Dolores Larkin said, reaching in and lifting it out. It was crumpled like it had been chewed.

'That probably belongs to the man who was eaten, Miss Larkin,' the Professor called.

'Urrgh, how creepy!' Dolores Larkin shrieked, dropping it in the boat by Ulf's feet. She spoke breathlessly into her voice recorder. 'A hat is all that remains of the dead man.'

Ulf tried to concentrate. There was definitely something large coming up; he could see the water stirring and bubbling around them. He pulled his hands clear, then suddenly felt his boat rising up in the air. The impossipus was surfacing right beneath the rowing boat, lifting it out of the water!

Suddenly the boat toppled, causing Ulf to lose his balance.

'Help!' Dolores Larkin cried, tipping out of the boat and splashing into the icy lake.

'Professor, help!' Ulf called, tumbling in headfirst after her.

CHAPTER SIX

Ulf gasped, swallowing a mouthful of water, the impossipus's tentacles writhing around him, its enormous body floating on the surface like a jelly island.

'It's got me!' Dolores Larkin cried, splashing and screaming as a huge tentacle wrapped around her. 'It's going to eat me!'

Ulf heard gasps from the crowd on the shore.

'The beast is attacking!' one man yelled.

Ulf swam towards the reporter to try to help her, but then a tentacle wrapped around him too. 'Professor, help!' he called, feeling its suckers grasping him. It lifted him from the water and he saw soldiers pointing their rifles from the shore.

Major Brigstock called through a megaphone, 'Ready, men! Aim—'

'Hold your fire!' the Professor called back. 'Please, stay calm, Ulf… Miss Larkin.'

The impossipus swung Ulf and Dolores Larkin round, looking up at them with its large stalk eyes.

Dolores Larkin was still screaming, 'Help! Help me!'

The beast's stalk eyes blinked, then to Ulf's surprise it gently lowered him and Dolores Larkin, placing them both back into the rowing boat.

'That's more like it, Tomiko,' the Professor said, reaching from his boat to stroke the beast.

The impossipus coiled a tentacle playfully around the Professor as he tickled its slimy suckers. 'You remember me, don't you, girl?'

Ulf sat up, shaken by what had happened.

'Tomiko's friendly,' the Professor said. 'She

was just checking you out. I told you she's usually good-natured.'

Ulf stared at the huge creature, puzzled. He could see hundreds of tentacles writhing beneath the water's surface, extending from its see-through jelly-like body, some feeling along the sides of the boats.

'Then how c-c-come she attacked and k-killed a citizen?' Dolores Larkin asked, shivering wet and in shock.

The Professor frowned. 'It's totally out of character, Miss Larkin. She's just a softie at heart. Give her a stroke if you like.'

Ulf reached from his boat and gently stroked one of the impossipus's tentacles. It softly bellowed.

'There you go. She likes you,' the Professor said. 'She was just a little startled earlier, weren't you, Tomiko?'

'I thought we were g-g-goners!' Dolores Larkin said. She shook herself, trying to dry her coat and mittens, and stared at the beast, surprised by its behaviour. 'N-not what I had expected a–a–at all.'

'Are you okay, Miss Larkin?' Ulf asked.

'I'm f–f–fine, I think,' the reporter replied.

'Ready to carry on, Ulf?' the Professor called.

Ulf wiggled his fingers in his ears to clear the water. 'Ready when you are, Professor.'

'Then let's harness this beast.'

Ulf had used a tentacle harness before, on a flaming squid in the seawater lagoon back at Farraway Hall, so he knew what to do.

Together he and the Professor rowed clear of the beast's long tentacles, bringing their boats side by side, then sunk the canvas cradle deep under the water, each keeping hold of its long straps. They rowed out on either side of the impossipus, dragging the cradle directly beneath the beast, then hoisted the straps, heaving the cradle into place underneath its body.

'If you want to secure the harness, Ulf, Tomiko's strong enough to stand on,' the Professor called. 'She won't mind.'

Tomiko's stalk eyes turned to look at Ulf as he stepped hesitantly from his rowing boat on to her island-like squidgy back. He could see right down into her see-through body: her large heart pumping and her grey brain spongy like an oversized cauliflower. Her belly was full of weed, eels and ducks... and a man's arm and leg, still wearing the remains of a suit.

Ulf gasped, shocked to see that the rumours were true. The impossipus *had* eaten the man. *But why, if it was good-natured?* he thought.

At that moment he heard the *thwock thwock thwock* of helicopter blades. He looked up and saw the RSPCB helicopter coming into view in the distance. 'Dr Fielding's on her way, Professor,' he said. But as Ulf fastened the harness's straps to a central ring that the flying cable could attach to, he noticed something shining by his foot. He bent down to take a closer look, and saw a bullet embedded in Tomiko's body! He saw two more beside it — three bullets in a cluster. '**Professor, Tomiko's been shot!**' he called, alarmed.

The Professor leaned from his boat with a look of great concern. 'Shot?' He stroked the impossipus. 'Tomiko, what happened to you?'

'Perhaps it was the soldiers,' Ulf said, glancing to the shore.

'Major Brigstock said she hadn't surfaced all morning,' the Professor reminded him.

'Perhaps it was the man she ate,' Dolores Larkin said. 'Maybe he shot her trying to defend himself.'

'Is that what happened, Tomiko?' the Professor said to the impossipus, continuing to stroke it. 'Just happened to have a gun, did he?' His voice sounded doubtful. 'This is most worrying,' he muttered, glancing around the lake, deep in thought.

'What are you thinking, Professor?' Ulf asked.

'I'm thinking that I'd like to know what

that man was doing out here in the middle of the night, Ulf. And why he would have had a gun with him. I don't think Tomiko would attack unless...' The Professor paused and looked up; the throbbing sound of helicopter blades was now loud overhead, the RSPCB helicopter hovering directly above.

'Unless what?' Ulf called, raising his voice trying to be heard, his hair blowing in all directions and spray from the lake swirling around him.

'Unless that man attacked Tomiko first!' the Professor shouted back.

Ulf heard Dolores Larkin trying to holler into her voice recorder, her voice smothered by the sound of the rotor blades: 'Shocking new development. Bullets found in beast. RSPCB suspicious.'

He reached up as the steel flying cable lowered from the helicopter, swinging in the downdraft. He saw Tiana sparkling beside it, guiding the cable down to the beast.

'Ulf, Dr Fielding says to hurry to Avenue

Six!' the fairy called in a fluster. 'There's another beast on the loose!'

'Another one?' Ulf asked surprised.

'I didn't realize there were more beasts in the city!' Dolores Larkin called.

'It's a slurper – a big one, Ulf,' Tiana replied. 'We saw it from the air on our way in. Dr Fielding's contacted Orson and he's bringing the beast transporter here to fetch it while she flies the impossipus back to Farraway Hall.'

'Right, Ulf, we'd better go,' the Professor announced, and he began rowing back in the direction of the shore.

Ulf fastened the flying cable to the metal ring at the top of the harness then ran back to his boat. 'Tiana, tell Dr Fielding that the impossipus needs surgery,' he called. 'She's been shot.'

'*Shot! How? When?*' The fairy gasped.

'Just take care of her,' Ulf called, as the helicopter lifted the impossipus out of the lake and up into the air.

'We will,' Tiana called, and she zoomed back up to the cockpit to tell Dr Fielding.

Ulf started rowing back, following the Professor as fast as he could.

'Events are moving rapidly,' Dolores Larkin said into her voice recorder. 'Word has just reached us of a second beast, called a slurper, on the loose in the city. The RSPCB are racing to recover it as we speak.'

At the shore Ulf saw the army dismantling their rifles, and the crowd looking up, watching the helicopter carry the impossipus away. He tied up his boat and grabbed the dead man's hat in case it could be a clue to his identity. He stuffed the hat into his bag then helped Miss Larkin out of the boat.

'Hurry, Ulf,' the Professor called, already running up the snowy shore to the RSPCB truck.

'I'll get my car and meet you both at Avenue Six,' Dolores Larkin said, her clothes still dripping wet.

'Sorry about the icy dip, Miss Larkin,'

Ulf replied. 'I hope you're not put off beasts for ever.'

'No, no, quite the opposite,' the reporter told him. 'It was fascinating – most educational. One beast caught, one more to go!'

'Did you hear that? There's another beast now too!' a man cried from the crowd.

Ulf hurried back to the RSPCB truck and climbed inside with the Professor as people came rushing forwards, calling out questions.

'How many more beasts have you been keeping secret?' one called.

'Will our city ever be safe again?' another yelled.

Ulf felt a little afraid as the crowd chanted: 'Protect humans, not beasts! Protect humans, not beasts!'

The Professor started the truck's engine. 'Ulf, one thing you'll learn as an RSPCB agent is that humans can be far trickier to handle than any beast,' he said. He beeped the truck's horn for the crowd to part and they sped out of the park.

Ulf glanced in the rear view mirror, still wondering about the gunshot wounds to the impossipus and what the man she'd eaten had been doing at the lake in the middle of the night.

CHAPTER SEVEN

Professor Farraway drove at top speed through the icy city streets heading for Avenue Six. He swerved to overtake traffic, beeping the truck's horn, while Dolores Larkin followed behind in her little blue car.

'Is the slurper an escapee from the old beast trade too, Professor?' Ulf asked.

'Yes, Ulf. Rumbold the slurper, as I named him, went to live in the city's sewers. He could be causing all kinds of trouble now that he's come above ground.'

Ulf opened *The Book of Beasts* and flicked to the entry **SLURPERS**:

Slurpers are enormous slug-like beasts with a very pungent odour. Commonly found in dark or damp habitats, they have voracious appetites but poor eyesight, and navigate by smell, sucking up anything in their path with their gummy toothless mouths then churning it in their cavernous stomachs.

'What I don't understand is: why now, Ulf?' the Professor said. 'Why, after all these years of remaining hidden, have both these beasts suddenly shown themselves?'

'It does seem a bit of a coincidence,' Ulf said.

'A coincidence? It seems suspicious to me.' The Professor beeped the truck's horn and Ulf glanced ahead. Traffic was at a standstill and humans were fleeing their cars, running back down the snowy street towards them, screaming and panicking.

'RSPCB needing to pass!' the Professor called from his open window. But there was no way through.

'Professor, look,' Ulf said, spotting Major Brigstock ahead of them shouting orders to soldiers through a megaphone.

'Spread out, men! Guns at the ready!'

Ulf and the Professor jumped from the truck and ran through the traffic and crowds. Ulf smelt a foul stench of rotten food and drains and, beyond the crowd, saw a brown, slug-like beast sliming over a burger van in the city's main square outside City Hall. The slurper was the size of a bus, and humans were cowering from it, holding their hands over their mouths, choking from its stench. With a mighty thud, the huge beast tipped the van over then pressed its blubbery face to the van's serving hatch like it was feeding from a bowl.

'Help! I'm trapped!' the burger seller called from inside.

'Marksmen at the ready,' Major Brigstock ordered. 'Fire on my command…'

'No, wait!' the Professor yelled.

But the beast was snuffling frantically, trying to get at the food inside the van.

The soldiers aimed their rifles.

'Don't shoot!' Ulf cried, sprinting towards the slurper, waving his arms to stop them, putting himself in the line of fire. He held his hand to his nose and mouth to keep out the stench, and leapt up on to the van to try and pull the burger seller out through the passenger door. But Rumbold the slurper's massive body blocked his way. Ulf pressed his shoulder to the beast's side, trying to push its slimy folds of fat out of the way. Gunk and slime squelched down his arm as he gripped the van's door handle and wrenched open the door.

The burger seller scrambled out to safety. 'Thank you,' he said gratefully to Ulf. 'I thought that thing was going to eat me!' And he hurried away into the crowd as quickly as he could.

The Professor came running over. 'Good work, Ulf!' he said.

Ulf coughed from the stench, watching Rumbold sucking out the contents of the van, swallowing every last thing: boxes of burgers and buns, sauce bottles and even cans of fizzy drink. The beast grunted and large boil–like protrusions on its face opened up, oozing with slime.

Ulf felt nauseous just being near the slurper. It was with relief that he heard the *honk! honk!* of the RSPCB transporter lorry coming to collect it. He looked across the crowd and saw the lorry trying to get through the jam of abandoned vehicles.

Orson was standing on the footplate at its back. 'Mind out of the way, everyone,' he called to the crowd.

The transporter lorry swerved one way then the other. Humans leapt aside as it mounted the pavement, knocking over a signpost then smashing a phone booth. It was being driven by Druce!

The gargoyle honked the transporter's horn and blew raspberries at the crowd through his window. 'Blurgh!' *HONK!* 'Blurgh!' *HONK!* 'Blurgh!' *HONK!*

The lorry skidded on slurper slime and

screeched to a halt a short distance from the beast.

'Nice driving, Druce,' Ulf said, giggling.

The gargoyle hopped up and down on his seat. 'Drucey coooool driver,' he gurgled.

Orson stepped down and opened the back of the transporter lorry, lowering its ramp to the ground. 'Right, let's get this beast out of here,' he said.

The slurper was sniffing the air, wanting more food. Ulf had an idea. He leaned into the van and pulled out a loose burger that had slipped down the side of the driver's seat. He reached up and waved the burger under the slurper's slimy nose. The beast sniffed it.

'Come and get it,' Ulf said, and he edged backwards towards the lorry.

'Good thinking, Ulf,' the Professor said.

Ulf waved the burger, continuing to the ramp at the back of the lorry. The beast followed, slobbering and drooling, its gummy mouth wafting rotten breath. Ulf threw the burger into the lorry's open back, and the beast began sliming up the ramp.

Orson rolled up his shirtsleeves and pushed the slurper's huge squidgy body the last few metres up the ramp, squeezing it safely inside. 'What a stinker!' the giant said, wrinkling his nose.

With the slurper safely on board, Orson closed the back of the transporter. 'Nice work, Ulf,' he said.

'Fur Face clever!' Druce gurgled, leaning from the lorry's window drooling, pretending he was a slurper too.

Ulf squeezed his T-shirt, wringing out stinky slime, and listened to contented snuffling and slurping sounds coming from inside the transporter.

'Right, Orson, you'd better get Rumbold back to Farraway Hall while we carry on checking things out here,' Professor Farraway said to the giant.

'You not coming with us, Professor?' Orson asked.

'Ulf and I will follow on later in the truck,'

the Professor replied.

Ulf knew that the Professor wanted to find out more about the suspicious nature of the beast attack.

'Okay, I'll see you back at Farraway Hall,' Orson said, and he stepped back up on to the lorry's footplate. Druce honked the horn and drove the beast transporter away through the crowds.

But people were still angry. 'Beasts out! Beasts out! Beasts out!' they chanted.

Dolores Larkin hurried over. 'Professor, the public deserve to know the truth,' she said. 'Why were these beasts being kept secret? Are there any more in the city?' She held her voice recorder up for him to speak into.

Ulf looked at the Professor anxiously, wondering if he was going to tell Dolores Larkin about the metamorphs that Dr Fielding had mentioned that morning.

'No, that's all of them now, Miss Larkin,' the Professor lied. 'Capitol City won't be troubled by beasts anymore…'

Ulf glanced around at the chaos that Rumbold had caused: upturned cars, spilled bins, knocked-over newsstands, and a stinky slime trail that oozed across the snowy ground to an abandoned underground station. Ulf went over to take a look, wondering if that was where Rumbold had come from. He saw the station's entrance gates had been bust open; there was a padlock lying broken on the ground. 'Professor, Miss Larkin, over here,' he called.

As the Professor and Dolores Larkin came to see, Ulf took a torch from his shoulder bag and shone it inside the entrance, lighting a slimy trail leading up a flight of steps from the darkness below.

'What have you found, Ulf?' the Professor asked.

'Follow me,' Ulf replied, heading down into the deserted station. He followed the trail along the train tracks to a large hole smashed into a tunnel wall. It lead into a sewer. He saw a sledgehammer lying on the ground by the hole. 'I don't think Rumbold broke out, Professor. I think someone let him out.'

'But why would anyone do that?' Dolores Larkin asked, mystified.

Professor Farraway paced anxiously up and down the tracks. 'What's been happening, I wonder? Two beasts causing mayhem in the space of a single day: one person dead, three bullets, and now a sledgehammer…'

'Are you suggesting that *humans* are responsible for all this?' Dolores Larkin asked.

'That's how it looks to me,' the Professor replied.

'But who? And why?'

Ulf reached into his bag and took out the hat he'd found at the lake. 'Professor, we could ask Dr Fielding to examine this hat for traces of DNA, to try and find out who that dead man was.'

'We may have to, Ulf,' the Professor replied.

Ulf checked the hat over, just in case the man had written his name inside, but all he could find was the maker's label. He shone his torch on it and read: 'FOXTON'S HATS, WILDCAT ALLEY.'

The Professor leaned down to Ulf's side. 'What was that you just said?'

'It's what's written on the label in the dead man's hat. I think it's the name of a shop.'

'May I see?' the Professor asked. Ulf handed him the hat and the Professor checked the label himself. 'Ulf, this isn't just any shop. This shop is in Wildcat Alley, the location of the old beast trade: it used to sell beast goods!'

The Professor raced back up the station's steps with the hat in his hand.

'Professor, where are you going?' Ulf called.

'Come on, Ulf! Come on, Miss Larkin! We're going to Wildcat Alley. We've some investigating to do!'

CHAPTER EIGHT

It was late in the afternoon and the sky was growing darker as Ulf and Professor Farraway sped through the city's backstreets, turning down an icy alleyway. Dolores Larkin followed behind.

'This, Ulf, is Wildcat Alley,' the Professor said, driving slowly over its snowy cobbles, glancing to shops on either side.

Ulf read their names: DE LAIG'S JEWELLERS... BENZENE'S PHARMACY... SPOON'S CAFÉ... SCRAG'S BAGS....

'These shops all used to sell beast goods and were owned by some extremely unpleasant people.'

The shops' windows looked tatty and uncared-for, and Ulf could see hardly any shoppers inside.

'Here we are,' the Professor said, parking in front of a shop called FOXTON'S HATS.

Ulf and the Professor stepped out, and Dolores Larkin parked up behind them.

The window to FOXTON'S HATS looked dusty. There were no lights on inside the shop and its sign read CLOSED.

Dolores Larkin stepped to Ulf's side, speaking into her voice recorder, 'The RSPCB visit Wildcat Alley on the trail of the dead man – the owner of the Foxton's hat.'

Professor Farraway tried the shop's door but it was locked. He knocked but there was no answer. He peered through the letterbox. 'Hello, is anyone in?' he called.

The shop seemed deserted.

Ulf glanced round, noticing a man in a blood-spattered apron watching them from a butcher's shop across the street. He was sharpening a carving knife.

'We're being watched,' Ulf whispered to the Professor, rolling his eyes in the direction of the man. 'He looks kind of scary.'

Professor Farraway peered in the window of FOXTON'S HATS, checking the man opposite by his reflection. 'That's Sam Enema, Ulf,' he whispered, 'the son of Ernie Enema who was once a beast butcher here. Sam was just a boy the last time I saw him. His dad's dead now. Nasty lot, the Enemas.'

The Professor turned and walked across the street towards the butcher. 'Good day,' he said. 'We're investigating the recent beast attack. We believe the victim may have connections to Foxton's hat shop. Have you seen the shopkeeper lately?'

The butcher ran his knife down his sharpener. 'Mr Foxton closed up an hour ago,' he said.

'And do you know where he might be now?'

The butcher smirked. 'Can't say I do.'

'Then I'm sorry to have troubled you.'

Professor Farraway smiled genially. He stepped away down the street, gesturing to Ulf and Dolores Larkin to follow him.

'He's lying,' the Professor whispered to them. 'Mr Foxton certainly didn't close up an hour ago. Through the letterbox of FOXTON'S HATS I saw this morning's newspaper still on the doormat. No one's been in there all day or it would have been picked up.'

'But why would the butcher lie, Professor?' Dolores Larkin asked.

'Act casual, Miss Larkin,' the Professor said. 'Let's take a look around.'

Ulf, Professor Farraway and Dolores Larkin strolled down Wildcat Alley glancing in shop windows. In MALONE'S FURNITURE, a man was stuffing cushions into a rubbish bin. In BENZENE'S PHARMACY, a man was emptying medicines into the sink, and in FOO'S SHOES, a woman was packing boots into boxes. All the shopkeepers seemed to be clearing their shelves of goods. Many of the shops' signs were turned to CLOSED.

In DEACON'S DRESSES, a woman was dusting the shop's mannequins. She glared at Ulf through the window.

'That's Mary Deacon,' the Professor whispered. 'Her mother used to sell beast-fur coats here.'

'Let me ask her if she's seen Mr Foxton,' Dolores Larkin said. 'I'll look less conspicuous than you in a ladies' dress shop.'

'Good thinking, Miss Larkin,' Ulf said.

As Dolores Larkin went to ask in the shop, Ulf and the Professor peered into FATCHUCK'S PIE SHOP next door. Behind the counter, a chubby woman was rolling out pastry.

'That's Jemima Fatchuck. Her mother Hattie Fatchuck used to sell beast pies,' the Professor whispered. He pushed on the door handle and Ulf followed him inside.

'We're closed,' the woman snapped.

'Actually, we're just looking for Mr Foxton, the owner of FOXTON'S HATS,' the Professor said. 'It's to do with the recent beast attack.

Do you know of his whereabouts?'

The woman sniggered. 'I believe he went on holiday,' she replied. Then she leaned over the counter and gave Ulf a sniff. She glanced at his bare hairy feet. 'You're a ripe one, aren't you?' she said, licking her fat red lips.

Ulf felt a shiver run up his spine and turned away. He noticed a slate propped up at the end of the counter with words written on it in chalk:

BEAST PIES
COMING AGAIN SOON

'Professor, look,' he whispered, signalling towards it with his eyes.

Miss Fatchuck quickly turned the sign face down on the counter. 'Oh, that's an old sign,' she said. 'I'm just having a clear out.'

But Ulf saw a stick of chalk poking out of her apron pocket. *That sign's not old; she's just written it*, he thought.

The Professor frowned. 'Well, thank you for your time, Miss Fatchuck. I guess we'll be off.'

As they left, Ulf whispered, 'She was lying, Professor. She just wrote that with the chalk in her pocket.'

'I know, Ulf. I saw it too,' the Professor replied. 'I don't like the look of this.'

They met Dolores Larkin coming out of the dress shop. 'The lady inside says that Mr Foxton has been away sick,' she told them. 'Do you think that can be true?'

'Miss Larkin, I think there's something very peculiar going on here,' Professor Farraway said, and they crossed the street to ask in some other shops.

Dolores Larkin went into WIGGINS' WIGS, and the Professor and Ulf headed into JACOB'S JAMS. A man in glasses was washing out jam jars in a sink at the back of the shop, stacking them into boxes.

'That's Alfred Jacobs, Ulf,' the Professor whispered. 'His father, Butch Jacobs, used to make beast jam.'

The shopkeeper turned. 'I was about to close up,' he said.

'We're from the RSPCB, Mr Jacobs. We've a few questions to ask, that's all,' the Professor said. 'We're looking for Mr Foxton. Have you seen him?'

Alfred Jacobs rubbed his chin. 'Hmm, Foxton. Nope, sorry, that name doesn't sound familiar.'

'How strange, because he owns the shop across the alley from you,' the Professor said sternly.

'Oh, *that* Foxton,' Alfred Jacobs smirked. 'Nope, ain't seen him lately.'

Ulf noticed a door open at the back of JACOB'S JAMS, and could see into a storeroom full from floor to ceiling with a huge metal contraption. It had two large iron slabs like bunk beds, one above the other, and cogs to move them up and down. He stepped over to take a closer look, but Alfred Jacobs slammed the door shut.

'Customers aren't allowed out back. It's private,' he said curtly.

The Professor opened the door again to

see. 'Hmm, what's a beast press doing here still, Alfred?'

Alfred Jacobs scowled. 'Oh, that old thing, that's been rusting out there for years. It's too heavy for me to move.'

The Professor fixed the shopkeeper with a stare. 'You had better not be up to anything illegal Mr Jacobs,' he said. Then he turned to Ulf. 'Come on, I think it's time we were leaving.'

'What was that machine?' Ulf whispered as they headed back out of the jam shop. 'Its cogs looked freshly oiled.'

'It's an old beast jam press,' the Professor replied. 'Used for turning beasts into jam. I'm not liking this one little bit.'

Ulf saw Miss Larkin going into SPOON'S CAFÉ, still investigating, and watched shopkeepers' faces up and down the street scowling from behind their shop windows. 'Everyone's behaving very suspiciously about Mr Foxton,' he said. 'Do you think it was *him* who was killed in the attack, Professor? Do you think *he* was going after the impossipus, to shoot it?'

'Maybe, Ulf, and that would mean that the shopkeepers of Wildcat Alley are up to their old evil ways again.' He glanced across the street at the darkened windows of FOXTON'S HATS. 'If Mr Foxton *was* the man killed, then I'd like to find out how he knew of the beast's secret whereabouts.'

A worrying thought entered Ulf's mind. 'Professor, you know you said that when you used to visit the city to check on the beasts, Marackai came with you...?'

The Professor's eyes widened. 'You don't think—'

'You two come with me,' a voice interrupted.

Ulf and Professor Farraway turned to see Sam Enema the butcher coming towards them.

'Someone wants a word with you,' he said. He had his butcher's knife in his hand.

Jemima Fatchuck the pie maker came over

too, then Jeremy Spoon the café owner and Alfred Jacobs the jam maker.

'Do as you're told, and don't make a scene,' Sam Enema said, marching Ulf and the Professor to his butcher's shop.

'Hey, hands off!' Ulf said.

'What's the meaning of this?' the Professor asked crossly.

But the shopkeepers jostled them inside, then pushed them into a refrigeration room at the back of the shop where frozen slabs of meat were hanging on hooks. 'Wait there.'

'Hey, what are you doi—'

The door to the refrigeration room slammed shut, then a moment later Ulf heard the shop's bell ring. He heard footsteps and whispering voices as someone spoke to the shopkeepers. The refrigeration room's door slowly opened again and a man in a long fur coat peered in, his face sneering and twisted like a rotten apple core.

Ulf gasped. 'Marackai!' he and the Professor both said, shocked.

'It's *Baron* Marackai to you. And your investigation stops right here!' The Baron grinned, then glanced over his shoulder to the shopkeepers. 'String them up!'

CHAPTER NINE

The shopkeepers held Ulf and the Professor, forcing their hands behind their backs and tying them with rope.

'Get off me!' Ulf yelled, trying to yank his arm free, but he felt the steel tip of Sam Enema's blade press to his side.

'I wouldn't struggle if I were you,' the butcher said.

'Or you might get hurt,' Jemima Fatchuck giggled, pulling the rope so tight that Ulf could feel it cutting into his skin. The shopkeepers lifted Ulf and the Professor off the ground and hung them on one of the large meat hooks dangling from the ceiling.

Baron Marackai sneered. 'So, Father, you're alive again, eh? Well, you won't be for long. And the same goes for you, werewolf.'

Ulf swung his legs, trying to kick the Baron, but the beast hunter dodged out of the way.

'You sent Mr Foxton after the impossipus, didn't you, Marackai?' the Professor said.

'Oh, you *have* been busy detectives,' Baron Marackai replied. 'Well, I wouldn't exactly say that I *sent* him. More dragged him, kicking and screaming. Then I shot a few bullets at that beast to make it angry and, *hey presto*, one dead citizen. The public is outraged.'

'You made the beast attack him!'

'Well, Mr Foxton didn't want to go along with my plans,' the Baron told them. 'He's far more use to me dead than alive, though: now the public hate beasts, just like in the old days. Ha ha!'

'What are you up to, Marackai?' the Professor asked.

'Haven't you noticed? I'm starting up the beast trade again, here in Wildcat Alley! Shame you won't be alive long enough to see it back in business.' The Baron pulled his fur coat tightly around him. 'Brrrrrr, chilly in here, isn't it? A person could freeze to death.' He laughed. 'Ha ha ha ha haaa!'

'You won't get away with this, Marackai,' Ulf said.

'Ah, but I will, werewolf, and now I'm off to hunt down all the metamorphs in this city too. They're what I *really* want — they're worth a fortune to me as beast goods.' He turned to the shopkeepers. 'Come on you lot, let's go.'

As they headed out of the door, Ulf called, 'Leave the metamorphs alone, Marackai.'

'Don't worry, Ulf,' the Professor told him. 'He'll never find them.'

The Baron poked his twisted face back in. 'Oh, won't I, Daddy? A crowd of frightened citizens is gathered outside City Hall as we speak, calling for an end to the RSPCB's secrecy. Imagine how angry they'll be when I tell them that there are metamorphs in their city too. I'm sure they'll help me root them all out.' He grinned. 'Right, must dash.' And he slammed the door shut.

Ulf struggled to free himself, but the ropes were tied tight. He could hear the Professor's teeth chattering from the cold. 'We have to g-get out of here and s-s-stop him.'

Ulf could feel the hairs on his arms starting to frost up. Even with his werewolf blood he wouldn't be able to withstand the refrigeration room's sub-zero temperatures for long. He wriggled and shook, trying to loosen the ropes around his wrists.

'It's n-n-no use, Ulf,' Professor Farraway said. 'We're seriously d-d-done for.' He called out loudly, 'Can anybody h-h-hear me? Help-p-p!'

Dolores Larkin! Ulf suddenly thought. *She'll be out there somewhere looking for us!* 'Miss Larkin, help us!' he called as loudly as he could. 'We're in the butcher's! We're trapped!'

The shop's bell rang – someone was coming in.

'Help! We're out the back!'

The door of the refrigeration room opened and Dolores Larkin peered inside. 'Oh, my gosh!' she exclaimed, seeing them strung up. 'What on earth happe—'

'Could you p-p-please get us down, Miss Larkin?' the Professor said. 'It's f-f-freezing in here.'

Dolores Larkin grabbed a box of frozen meat and stood on it to unhook them. 'All the shopkeepers just went running off up the street,' she said. 'What happened to you?'

'It was Marackai,' Ulf explained. 'He did it.'

'Who's Marackai?' Dolores Larkin asked, confused.

The Professor and Ulf dropped to the ground, their hands freed. They staggered out of the refrigeration room to warm up in the shop. 'M-M-Marackai's my son. He tied us up in here,' the Professor said.

'Your son?'

'He's a beast hunter,' Ulf explained. 'It was him who shot the impossipus and made it attack that man. He's trying to make the public hate beasts so he can go after the metamorphs.'

'Metamorphs? And what are they?' Dolores Larkin asked, looking more bewildered by the second.

Ulf and the Professor rubbed their bodies to get their blood circulating again.

'Miss Larkin, I'm sorry but I've not been totally honest with you,' Professor Farraway said. 'There *are* more beasts in Capitol City. Metamorphs are humanoid transforming beasts that live among the public. I didn't tell you about them earlier because I feared it might jeopardise their safety if people knew of them.'

'And now we have to stop Marackai before he finds them,' Ulf said, hurrying out of the shop. The Professor and Miss Larkin followed.

Outside, Wildcat Alley was now eerily

quiet. The shopkeepers had all left with Marackai, and the evening sky was almost dark, with night now closing in.

'Come on,' the Professor called, rushing to the truck. **_WE HAVEN'T A MOMENT TO LOSE!_**

BEASTLY
BUSINESS

CHAPTER TEN

Ulf and Professor Farraway sped off in the truck in pursuit of Marackai, following the route back towards the public demonstration outside City Hall. Half way there, the Professor screeched the truck to a halt and pulled over in a dark back street surrounded by tall apartment blocks.

'Why are we stopping here?' Ulf asked.

'This is where you get out, Ulf,' Professor Farraway replied.

Ulf looked at the Professor, confused. 'Get out?'

'If Marackai has already told the public about the metamorphs then the city will be too dangerous for them to stay in, and you'll be in danger too,' Professor Farraway explained. 'We need to get them all out. I'll head to the city centre to try to stop Marackai while you round up the metamorphs and head to safety.'

'*Me?* But how?'

'You won't be alone, Ulf. I'm hoping we'll find an old friend of mine here to help you.' Professor Farraway stepped out of the truck and looked up at an apartment block, cupping his hands to his mouth. He hooted into the dark evening sky like an owl, '*Twit Twoo. Twit Twit Twit. Twoo Twoo Twoo.*'

Dolores Larkin parked behind the truck and walked over to Ulf's window. 'What's he doing?' she whispered.

'I'm not sure,' Ulf replied.

The Professor called again, '*Twit Twoo. Twit Twit Twit. Twoo Twoo Twoo.*'

Ulf heard a sound from high above. '*Twoo Twoo Twoo. Twit Twit Twit.*' It sounded like an owl replying. He noticed a man high up on the balcony of the apartment block.

Suddenly the man leapt off and plummeted down through the air.

'Woah! He's jumped!' Dolores Larkin cried, alarmed.

But as she spoke, wings appeared from the man's back and he swooped down, silhouetted against the dark sky, circling silently. *He's a metamorph!* Ulf realised.

The metamorph landed beside the Professor in the dark back street, folding his wings to his sides. Close up, he looked like some kind of owl-man, with large round eyes, a feathered face and a hooked nose like a beak. 'I haven't heard that greeting call in years, Professor,' he said. 'It's good to see you.'

'It's good to see you too, Al,' the Professor replied. 'It's been a long time.'

Ulf and Dolores Larkin stared, astonished, as the metamorph's wings receded into slits in his jacket, and the feathers on his face disappeared into his skin – he was turning back into his human form.

'I didn't realise you were still alive, Professor,' Al said.

'It's a long story,' Professor Farraway replied. 'And I'm afraid there's no time to chat.'

The man's head swivelled like an owl's, looking at Ulf and Dolores Larkin. 'Who are these two?'

'Friends,' the Professor said, leading him to one side. 'Listen, I need to ask you a favour…'

Professor Farraway turned his back on Ulf and whispered into the owl-man's ear. Ulf saw Al look back at him, then nod to the Professor. The two men shook hands warmly.

'Right then,' Professor Farraway said. 'Ulf, Al will help you gather the metamorphs. Miss Larkin and I will look for Marackai.'

'Are you sure about this?' Ulf asked nervously, stepping from the truck.

'Trust me, Ulf. You can do this. We'll meet you at midnight at the Williamson Bridge exit road out of the city, then we'll drive the metamorphs to the safety of Farraway Hall.'

Dolores Larkin spoke into her voice

recorder, 'Night is falling, and the RSPCB boy is to search for the elusive metamorph beasts.'

The Professor climbed back into the RSPCB truck, and Dolores Larkin hurried back to her car. 'Good luck, Ulf,' she called.

As the Professor and Dolores sped off to look for Marackai, Ulf glanced at Al. 'Where shall we start?' he asked. 'Do you know where the other metamorphs live?'

The owl-man smiled, his face turning feathery again, and his wings sprouting from the slits in his jacket. He spread them wide. 'Climb on, Ulf. I'll take you to them.'

Ulf climbed on to Al's back and gripped hold of his feathers. The owl-man flapped his wings, and they took off into the sky.

CHAPTER ELEVEN

Ulf clung on tightly as Al soared up through the night sky. The owl-man beat his powerful wings, lifting Ulf high above the streets and rooftops until they were soaring over the city skyscrapers. With just a gentle flick of his wingtips, Al was able to manoeuvre skilfully through the air.

Ulf looked down in awe at the city below, the lights of windows like tiny yellow stars in the dark.

'You okay, Ulf?' Al asked.

'I think so,' Ulf replied, nervous in case he fell.

'Hold on tight,' Al said, and he dived down

through the darkness to a wharf where boats were moored. He swooped low above the water, landing on a wooden jetty beside a large houseboat.

'This is our first stop, Ulf. Home to Fred the froglanoid.'

Al transformed back into his human form and called, 'Fred, are you there? It's Al. There's someone here to see you.'

Ulf heard the sound of shuffling from inside the boat's cabin. Its door opened and out stepped a bald-headed man with strange scars on his neck.

'What's up?' the man asked, then he looked at Ulf in surprise.

'I'm Ulf,' Ulf said, trying to sound more confident than he felt. 'I'm from the RSPCB.'

Fred the froglanoid glanced down quizzically at Ulf's bare hairy feet.

'The city's not safe for metamorphs at the moment,' Ulf went on. 'There's a beast hunter looking for you. You're all to meet by the Williamson Bridge at midnight to leave the city. Everyone's going back to RSPCB headquarters for safety.'

'I'll get going straight away,' Fred said. He kicked off his slippers and stepped down on to the dockside. Ulf noticed his feet were large and webbed. 'I'll tell the marsh banshees on my way.'

Fred's skin turned slimy and green. The scars in his neck opened, changing into gills, and his eyes moved to the sides of his face. 'It's good to see you again, Ulf,' he said, a long tongue flicking from his mouth. He dived into the water and with one kick he was gone.

See me again? Ulf thought, thinking the froglanoid must be mistaken. *But we've only just met.*

'Come on, Ulf. We've many more metamorphs to gather before midnight,' Al said. 'Next stop, Charna the spidrax.'

As Al turned back into his winged form, Ulf climbed on to his shoulders and they flew up into the sky. They soared over a grimy industrial part of the city and looked down on dark warehouses with smashed windows and overgrown yards where the snow lay deep and undisturbed.

They swooped down to one of the warehouses and in through a door that was hanging off its hinges. The warehouse looked derelict, with large cobwebs strung across its rafters. Ulf could see bats trapped among them.

'Charna, are you here?' Al called.

'Who isssss it?' a shrill voice hissed from above.

'Al. And Ulf from the RSPCB.'

Ulf looked up among the webs and saw a metamorph beast with eight spidery legs creeping down towards them. It dropped to the floor, transforming into a woman wearing a black silk robe.

She touched Ulf's furry cheek. 'Tsssss, haven't you grown,' she said.

Ulf smiled awkwardly at the woman. 'We've never met before,' he replied, wondering what she meant, and he explained why they'd come.

'I'll seeee you at the bridge at midnight,' Charna replied, and she shot a spider's thread from her hand and scuttled up to a web.

Ulf and Al took off to look for more metamorphs. This time they flew down to a small café on a quiet street corner.

'This is where Zena lives,' Al said.

The café was closing up and its owner, Zena, a woman with green eyes and thick black hair, was stacking chairs on tables. Ulf introduced himself and told her about the plan to evacuate to Farraway Hall.

Zena's ears twitched. 'Quiet a second, Ulf,' she whispered. Fangs pushed from her lips, and whiskers sprouted from her cheeks. Suddenly she pounced to the corner of the room, and there was a loud squeak followed by silence. Zena sat up with a huge rat in her jaws and gobbled it whole, sucking its tail down like spaghetti. 'Pesky little blighters. They're always getting into my cafe,' she said.

Ulf smiled, realising she was a werecat. 'We'll see you at midnight at the Williamson bridge exit road,' he said.

'I'll be there, Ulf,' Zena replied. 'And thanks.'

Ulf took off once more with Al to go and tell the others.

From Zena's café they flew to a city suburb, landing on a snowy pavement outside a row of houses.

'House number sixty-seven is where Varva the lavaman lives,' Al told Ulf.

They knocked on the door and a man with veiny, tanned skin peered out. As soon as Ulf introduced himself, the man smiled. 'Ulf! Well, I never,' he said. 'You must be freezing flying around in this weather. Do you two want to warm up?'

Ulf was a little taken aback by the man's friendliness. 'We haven't time to come inside,' he replied.

'Oh, there's no need to come in,' Varva said. At that moment his skin started to glow red-hot like lava, radiating super-warm heat.

'That's amazing!' Ulf said. And as he explained what had happened, he and Al warmed themselves from Varva's body heat. Then as Ulf was leaving, Varva the lavaman smiled once more.

'It's great to see you again, Ulf,' he said. 'It's been a long time.'

Ulf looked at the lavaman, confused. 'But we've not met before,' he replied.

Varva the lavaman winked. 'I'll see you both at the bridge at midnight.' And he closed the door.

As Ulf and Al took off once again, Ulf tugged Al's feathers. 'Al, how come the metamorphs are all acting like they know me?'

Al swivelled his head and smiled. 'You've forgotten, haven't you, Ulf?'

'What do you mean?'

'You were born here, in Capitol City.'

'I was?'

Ulf knew nothing of his distant past, only

that he'd been brought into the RSPCB rescue centre as a werecub when he was one month old.

Al soared higher, safely out of sight of any humans who might be looking up from the streets below. 'It was long ago, Ulf, but you lived here with your parents. Powerful werewolves, they were.'

'What happened to them, Al? How come I ended up at the RSPCB?'

Al flew silently for a moment as if he was choosing his words carefully. 'All us metamorphs used to meet from time to time in a disused factory several miles from here – good times, they were. Then one night, ten years ago, there was a fire. We never knew how it started, but the building's exit had been blocked from the outside and no one could escape.'

Ulf felt alarmed by what he was hearing. He clung on tightly, bracing himself.

'Your parents transformed and with wolf strength they smashed a hole in the wall. Your mother carried you out, then they both came back through the smoke to guide the rest of us to safety. They must have come back into that burning factory a dozen times trying to rescue us all. The building collapsed as they searched inside for the last of us: a banshee and an imp. They died, Ulf.'

Ulf felt numb with shock.

Al swivelled his head again to look back at Ulf. 'You okay? No one's ever told you this, eh?'

Ulf shook his head.

'Your parents were brave, Ulf; the bravest I've known. They died trying to save others.'

Al flicked his wings and banked around a skyscraper, and Ulf thought about everything he'd been told. He felt sad hearing about the death of his parents, but proud to know they had died heroes.

★ ★ ★

Meanwhile, Professor Farraway and Dolores Larkin had arrived in the square outside City Hall. Hundreds of people were gathered, demonstrating against beasts. They stepped from their vehicles and pushed through the crowd, looking around for Marackai and the Wildcat Alley shopkeepers.

Citizens were talking angrily to each other. 'Have you heard there are more beasts in the city?' one complained. 'Metamorphs! Beasts trying to pass themselves off as humans! The RSPCB never told us!'

The Professor looked across the crowd hearing a voice blare through a megaphone: 'Let's get the metamorphs now!' It was quite dark, but he could just make out Sam Enema the butcher calling from the steps of City Hall, a megaphone in his hand. The other shopkeepers from Wildcat Alley were with him.

'Let's root them out!' Jemima Fatchuck yelled to the crowd.

'Let's finish them off once and for all,' Mary

Deacon the dress shop owner cried.

Professor Farraway and Dolores Larkin pushed towards them. 'Where's Marackai?' the Professor demanded.

'You're meant to be locked in my freezer!' Sam Enema said, shocked to see the Professor.

'Tell me where my son is!' the Professor insisted. He glanced round looking for Marackai, but couldn't see him anywhere.

'You'll never find him,' Sam Enema sneered. 'He's too clever for you! Ha ha!'

'Beasts out!' Jemima Fatchuck shouted.

'Beasts out!' Alfred Jacobs cried.

The Professor and Dolores Larkin felt themselves being jostled by the crowd as the shopkeepers stepped down to lead the public off in search of the metamorphs.

'Beasts out! Beasts out! Beasts out!' the crowd chanted.

'What are we going to do now, Professor?' Dolores Larkin asked.

Professor Farraway was still looking for

Marackai, but could see no sign of him among the crowd. '*LET'S JUST HOPE ULF GETS TO THE METAMORPHS IN TIME.*'

CHAPTER TWELVE

On and on across the city Ulf and Al flew looking for the metamorphs, swooping over shut-up shops and offices, taxis and night buses, high streets and suburbs.

They visited an office block where a Transylvanian half-blood vampire was working as a night watchman, then a small terraced house where a family of myrmidon ant-people lived. They found a vipon snake woman with a forked tongue, a moscallon fly-man and a blue-skinned frostbreather. They spent ten minutes ringing the doorbell of a sleepy groan builder who grumpily came to the door in his bearlike beast form. Most of them recognised Ulf and remembered his parents too. It made Ulf proud knowing his parents had saved so many lives.

With the hour approaching midnight, Ulf and Al flew to the Williamson Bridge, the main bridge leading out of town. At its far end Ulf saw the RSPCB truck waiting in a lay-by on the side of the road with Dolores Larkin's little blue car parked behind it. The tarpaulin shelter was pulled up over the back of the truck and a whole gang of metamorphs were huddled together inside.

Al landed and Ulf jumped down and ran to the Professor, who was standing by the truck looking at his watch.

'Well done, Ulf,' the Professor said. 'It looks like your mission was a success.'

'Did you find Marackai?' Ulf asked.

'We searched everywhere but there was no sign of him. The shopkeepers have been busy though, stirring up the public against the metamorphs. The city's a dangerous place tonight.'

'Everyone's here,' Al said.

'Right then, let's go,' Professor Farraway replied.

Al hopped in the back of the truck with the others and Ulf climbed into the front beside the Professor.

As they sped off, Ulf could hear the metamorphs chatting in the back. 'Professor, Al told me about my past,' he said.

'I'm sorry about your parents, Ulf,' Professor Farraway replied. 'Dr Fielding told me this morning. She was worried about how you'd take it.'

'They were heroes,' Ulf said.

The Professor ruffled Ulf's hair. 'And so will you be once we've got this lot to safety tonight.'

In the side mirror, Ulf saw Dolores Larkin following in her car. 'Is Dolores coming too?' he asked.

'Miss Larkin's had a brilliant idea. She's going to write all about the RSPCB in tomorrow's newspaper, telling the public the truth about the city beasts and everything that's happened. She wants to help get the public back on our side, and teach them not to be afraid of beasts.'

'And what about Marackai? Who's going to look for him?'

'We'll contact NICE. They'll find him, Ulf.'

Ulf had heard of NICE before – the department for National and International Criminal Emergencies. He smiled. 'So everything's going to be okay now?'

'It certainly looks that way.'

Ulf leaned out of the window into the cold night air, 'Farraway Hall, here we come!'

CHAPTER THIRTEEN

On was the middle of the night by the time Ulf and Professor Farraway arrived back at the rescue centre. They turned down the driveway, and the Professor flashed the truck's headlights.

From the rooftop of Farraway Hall, Druce scampered down and opened the gates to let them in.

'Where you been? Drucey worry,' the gargoyle gurgled.

Ulf leaned from his window as the truck drove in. 'We're okay, Druce. We've just brought some friends to stay the night here,' he said, not wanting to alarm the gargoyle.

Druce hopped up and down excitedly seeing the metamorphs in the back of the truck. 'Morphy beasts – yeah!'

As Dolores Larkin parked up behind, he licked her windscreen with his long yellow tongue. 'Blurgh Blurgh! And lady beast too!'

Ulf stepped out, seeing Tiana whizzing across the yard and Dr Fielding hurrying from the house.

'What kept you?' Tiana asked.

'How come you've brought the metamorphs here?' Dr Fielding asked.

'It's not safe for them in the city,' Ulf explained. 'Marackai's there.'

'Marackai?' Tiana and Dr Fielding both exclaimed, startled.

Professor Farraway came to join them. 'I'm afraid it's true,' he said.

While the Professor explained everything that had happened in the city, Ulf noticed Dolores Larkin having trouble getting out of her little blue car.

Druce was leaning down from the roof of

the car licking her face as she tried to speak into her voice recorder. 'It's night time at Farraway Hall,' she said. 'The metamorphs arrive safely… urgh, stop that. The gates are locked… urrrgh!'

Ulf giggled.

Dolores Larkin came over, wiping Druce's sticky spit from her face. 'Hello, Dr Fielding I presume,' she said. 'If it's quite all right with you, I'd like to write an article in the *City Gazette* about all the good work the RSPCB does.'

'No problem, Miss Larkin,' Dr Fielding replied. 'If you'll come with me, we'll get everyone inside where they'll be safe, then I'll answer any questions you may have.'

Professor Farraway began leading the metamorphs into the house. 'This way,' he called. 'There are plenty of rooms upstairs. You'll all be quite comfortable here for the night.'

While the others went into the house for the night, Ulf and Tiana headed into the yard to say hello to Orson and to check on the beasts. Ulf breathed in the cold night air, tinged with the familiar aroma of beasts, and felt pleased to be back home. The door to the big beast barn was open and the light from Orson's lantern spilled out on the snow.

Ulf found the giant inside with Rumbold the slurper, kneeling beside it, massaging its belly. 'Hi, Orson.'

'Guess what, Orson?' Tiana said, zipping to the giant's light. 'We're going to be front page news tomorrow!'

'Really?' Orson asked. 'How come?'

'There's a reporter here. She's going to write all about us.'

Ulf coughed as a putrid stench rose from the slurper beast.

'Oh, excuse the smell, Ulf,' Orson said, wafting the air with his hand. 'I think Rumbold here's eaten rather too much. He's got tummy troubles.'

Ulf glanced back at the house, seeing lights in the windows of the upstairs bedrooms where the metamorphs were settling down to sleep. 'The metamorphs are staying here tonight, Orson,' he said. 'Marackai's in the city. It's not safe for them there.'

'Marackai! I should have guessed when I saw those bullets in old Tomiko.'

'How's the impossipus doing now?' Ulf asked.

'She's on the mend. I put her in the freshwater lake to rest.'

Ulf felt relieved that all the city beasts were now safe from Marackai. And thanks to Dolores Larkin, tomorrow the public would learn the truth about beasts.

'What do you say I put a word in for you with Dr Fielding, Ulf, to see if she'll let you have a little moonjuice tomorrow, so you can go wild with the metamorphs?'

'Yes, please!' Ulf said. Dr Fielding kept a bottle of moonjuice in her laboratory. It was the nectar of a night-flowering jungle plant and, like the full moon, could trigger a werewolf transformation.

'Thought you'd say that,' the giant replied smiling. 'Well, I think I'll tuck down now. It's been a long day.' He picked up his lantern then stepped out of the big beast barn, closing the door softly behind him so that Rumbold could rest. 'Night all,' he said and strode off to the feed store, to the mound of grain that he used for a bed.

'See you in the morning, Orson,' Ulf said. He waited for the giant to move out of ear-shot then turned to Tiana and whispered, 'Come with me a minute. I've got something to tell you.'

'What is it, Ulf?' the fairy asked.

Ulf strolled down the side of the paddock. 'I found something out today about my past – something that I'd never known before.'

As Ulf headed to the privacy of his den to tell Tiana his news, he glanced round in the darkness at the snow-covered beast park, seeing the silhouettes of beasts down in the paddock. He heard Druce gurgling on his perch on the rooftop of Farraway Hall, and

CHAPTER FOURTEEN

A short while later, in a dark fleshy chamber, Blud and Bone were sloshing up to their armpits in a cold mix of half-digested hamburgers, sausages and vile-smelling juices.

'It's 'orrible in here,' Bone said, shining a torch. The walls of the chamber were churning and rippling.

'It's part of the plan,' Blud said, checking his wristwatch. 'One more minute and we'll get out.'

'How are we going to do that?' Bone asked.

Blud pulled a packet from his jacket pocket. He shone his torch on it to illuminate the words: LAXATIVE – *shifts any blockage.*

Bone glanced down through the disgusting smelly juices at a pulsating hole in the chamber wall. 'You mean we're going out *that* way?' he said.

'Time to move,' Blud replied, emptying the contents of the packet into the juices and stirring them with his hand.

The walls of the chamber began squeezing inwards and foul gases bubbled up around them. The contents of the chamber sloshed and swirled like a whirlpool. All of a sudden, the pulsating hole in the chamber wall widened and they were sent whirling round and round in the disgusting juices as the liquid began draining away like water down a plughole.

'I don't wanna go this way!' Bone called nervously.

'*Too laaaaaaaaaaaaaaaaaate!*'

The two men were sucked through the hole and sent shooting down a slimy brown tunnel.

'Wooooah!'

They were squirted out through a tight opening on to the straw-covered floor of a barn, brown stinky liquid pouring out on top of them.

'Phwoar!' Bone said.

Blud put his finger to his lips. 'Shhh.'

They had come out from the rear end of Rumbold the slurper beast. The beast was groaning.

Blud wiped his face and got to his feet. He stepped to the barn door and peered out at a large country house. 'We're here,' he whispered. 'Farraway Hall.'

Quietly, Bone unzipped the holdall that was slung over his shoulder and took out a tranquiliser gun. 'Let's get to work.'

Both men edged nervously past the slurper beast and crept outside into the yard.

The sound of snoring was coming from a feed store a short distance away, and they tiptoed towards it.

'Ha ha, the giant's asleep,' Bone said, seeing Orson inside.

'Shh, keep your voice down,' Blud whispered.

But they'd been heard – Orson opened one eye. 'Oi, where did you come fr—'

Bone fired, shooting tranquiliser darts at the giant – *thwit, thwit, thwit, thwit* – three in his neck and one in his nose.

Orson fell back on to the mound of grain, unconscious.

Blud sniggered. 'Who's next?'

They turned, seeing a light on in Dr Fielding's office. The window was slightly open and she was sitting at her desk talking to Dolores Larkin.

'How about the vet?' Blud said.

They crept nearer. Dr Fielding was dialling a number on her phone. Dolores Larkin was coming to the window.

Suddenly, a gurgled voice called from above, 'Blurgh! Intruders! Blurgh!'

'Oh heck, we've been spotted!' Bone cried.

Druce was up on the rooftop, blowing raspberries and pulling faces at them.

Blud quickly fired a tranquiliser dart.

'Blu—'

It hit Druce on the nose, silencing him. He tumbled from the rooftop and fell all the way to the ground.

CHAPTER FIFTEEN

Ulf woke in his den. 'Tiana, what was that sound?' he asked.

But the fairy was fast asleep in the straw beside him.

He gave her a nudge. 'Tiana, wake up, I heard something. It sounded like Druce.'

The fairy woke, bleary-eyed. 'Ulf, go back to sleep,' she said.

Ulf looked out through the bars of his den, but couldn't spot the gargoyle on the rooftop. Concerned, he got up and ran out into the snow to see.

Tiana whizzed out after him. 'Ulf, what are you worrying about?'

In the yard by the house, Ulf saw Druce lying motionless in the snow.

'Druce, are you okay?' he called, running over.

But the gargoyle didn't move. He had turned to stone and was unconscious, a tranquiliser dart protruding from his nose. Then Ulf saw Orson fast asleep in the feed store with darts in him too.

'Over here, Ulf,' Tiana said, peering into Dr Fielding's office.

The doctor's window was open and she was slumped over her desk with two tranquiliser darts embedded in her neck.

Dolores Larkin came hurrying out of the side door with Professor Farraway. 'I saw them: two men with a gun,' the reporter said.

'What two men?' Ulf asked.

'They were out here,' Dolores Larkin told him, looking shaken. 'One big and one small. They came into the house and I ran to get the Professor.'

'Where are they now?' Ulf asked. Glancing

inside the house, he saw wet footprints leading up the back stairs. 'Professor, look,' he said, pointing to them.

'Oh heavens, the metamorphs are upstairs,' Professor Farraway replied. 'They could be in danger! Follow me!'

Ulf hurried after the Professor. They followed the footprints up the back stairs to the spare bedrooms on the second floor where the metamorphs were staying the night.

Ulf opened the first bedroom door and turned the light on. He saw Charna the spidrax woman unconscious with a tranquiliser dart in her neck. Then in the next room he found Freddie the froglanoid darted too. At the far end of the corridor he heard noises, two men were whispering in the end room, 'Let me do it.'

'No, it's my turn to be the shooter. Let me.'

Ulf and the Professor ran towards the sound then heard a *thwit!* They looked into the end room and through the gloom could just make out Al unconscious with a dart in his chest, and two men standing at the foot of his bed, one big and one small.

Ulf quickly lunged for them, snatching a rifle from the smaller man's hand. He kicked the big man in his shin, and the Professor picked up a bedpan from the end of the bed and whacked him with it.

Dolores Larkin and Tiana hurried in, and the little fairy's sparkles lit up the room.

'It's Marackai's henchmen!' Tiana cried, recognising Blud and Bone. She blasted the two men with her sparkles.

'Ow!' went the small man.

'Ooo!' the big man groaned.

Dolores Larkin joined in, slapping both their faces. 'You nincompoops!' She snatched the rifle from Ulf and pointed it at the big man.

'Dart him, Miss Larkin,' Tiana said. 'Pull the trigger!'

'No, please don't, Sir,' Blud said.

Sir? Ulf thought.

'Blud, Bone, must I do everything myself?'

Dolores Larkin said. Her voice sounded different, deeper somehow. She turned and pointed the gun at Ulf and the Professor.

'What's going on?' Ulf asked. 'What are you doing, Miss Larkin?'

The reporter smiled. 'Haven't you guessed?' She pulled off one of her woollen mittens and wriggled a fleshy stump where her little finger should have been.

'Marackai!' Ulf gasped, his blood running cold at the sight. 'But you can't be. You're a woman!'

'Can't I?' With the gun in one hand, Dolores Larkin pulled her hair with the other. It came off like a wig. 'Courtesy of WIGGINS' WIGS,' she said. Then she dug her fingers into the skin of her neck and pulled. The skin lifted away, peeling back from her face like rubber, revealing a man's face beneath, twisted with hatred like a rotten apple core. 'Fooled you, ha!'

Professor Farraway was incensed. '**YOU DESPICABLE, DISHONEST, WORTHLESS–**'

Baron Marackai pulled the trigger and a tranquiliser dart struck the Professor's ear. He slumped to the ground, unconscious.

Ulf leapt for the Baron, trying to knock the gun from his hand, and succeeded in slamming him against the wall.

'Bone, seize the werewolf, you buffoon!' Baron Marackai cried.

Ulf felt the big man grip his arms tightly from behind. He kicked and struggled, but Bone just squeezed tighter.

'I've got you, werewolf.'

'Let him go!' Tiana cried, blasting the big man with her sparkles. But Ulf heard a sickening *WHACK!* as Blud hit the fairy with the bedpan, sending her spinning to the floor, out cold.

Ulf glared at Baron Marackai. 'This is my home and these are my friends,' he said. 'Leave them alone!'

'Actually, I think you'll find that Farraway Hall is mine now,' the Baron replied. 'Along with all the beasts in it. And tomorrow I'm going to have a big beast sale that will close down the RSPCB for good.'

'A big beast sale!' Ulf exclaimed, sick with dread.

'Oh, yes. And the metamorphs will be my star items,' the Baron gloated. 'It was so much easier to capture them with your help than the last time I tried: ten years ago I set a little fire in the city but the blasted beasts escaped somehow.'

Ulf felt a fierce rage rise inside him. 'My parents died in that fire trying to save everyone! And *you* started it!'

Baron Marackai chuckled. 'Well, it's their fault for trying to be brave. Now, you wouldn't be so foolish, would you?'

Ulf tried to punch and kick the Baron, but Bone was still gripping him.

'Oh, let's not get in a twist about the past when there's such a glorious future to look forward to,' the Baron said. 'Think about it: the public now hate beasts, your friends will soon be dead and the RSPCB will be all but a fading memory. The beasts here will be turned into goods and sold in the city. Doesn't that sound splendid? I shouldn't even be surprised if tomorrow's newspaper reports how the great Baron Marackai saved the city from beasts.'

Ulf heard a *thwit!* as the Baron pulled the trigger. He felt a pain in his chest and looked down to see a tranquiliser dart embedded in his T-shirt.

Ulf pulled the dart out, but it was too late. Some of the tranquiliser had already entered his bloodstream. He felt woozy, then everything went black.

CHAPTER SIXTEEN

Ulf's head ached and his body felt heavy. He opened one eye and saw metal bars with daylight streaming in and snowflakes falling outside. He was in a cage, coming round from the effects of the tranquiliser. Groggily, he got to his feet and looked out.

The cage stood on top of a large metal contraption in the paddock of the beast park. He gasped, seeing his friends trapped too and still unconscious: Orson lying between the huge metal slabs of a jam press like the one in JACOB'S JAMS in Wildcat Alley; Tiana in a glass jar on a machine with wires and dials, and Druce chained to pegs in the ground with a cement mixer on a platform above him.

Out in the beast park, humans were driving vehicles across the snow: tractors and trailers, trucks, vans and lorries. Some were parked beside the beast enclosures with their human drivers peering in at the beasts.

It's the shopkeepers of Wildcat Alley, Ulf realised. He recognised Jemima Fatchuck the pie seller standing by the aviary as she winched a tranquilised griffin into the back of a truck. Sam Enema the butcher was towing a tranquilised yeti out of the snow dome with his meat van.

'Feel free to browse,' Ulf heard a voice blare from a megaphone. It was Baron Marackai, calling from the RSPCB Jeep, driving from the biodomes towards Farraway Hall. 'EVERYTHING MUST GO, LADIES AND GENTLEMEN. GET OUT YOUR WALLETS! THE BIG BEAST SALE IS OPEN FOR BUSINESS!'

From all around came cheering and the beeping of horns.

'Ah, and here come the star items,' the Baron announced.

Ulf saw the RSPCB truck trundling from the yard being driven by Blud. In its back the unconscious metamorphs were piled in a heap. Bone walked behind the truck dragging them off one at a time then tying them to the paddock fence posts.

'I'll buy the owl-man,' shouted Tony Malone the furniture seller from the cab of a lorry. 'I'll stuff my sofas with his feathers and turn his talons into coat hooks.'

'I'll buy the werecat woman,' Lily De Laig the jeweller called. 'I'll use her green eyes to make brooches!'

'I'll take the froglanoid,' shouted Jeremy Spoon the café owner. 'I'll chop off his legs and boil them for frogs' legs soup.'

Baron Marackai chuckled. 'I shall sell to the highest bidder,' he called from the RSPCB Jeep. 'Just as soon as I've attended to a small personal matter of my own.'

The Baron came driving across the

paddock towards Ulf and his friends. He parked nearby and looked up at Ulf in the cage. 'Ah, werewolf, awake already? So, what do you think of my big beast sale?'

'You won't get away with this, Marackai!' Ulf yelled down.

The Baron jumped down on to the snow. 'And who's going to stop me – the RSPCB? I think not.'

Marackai stepped over to Orson in the jam press. 'Wakey, wakey, Mr Giant,' he said, rubbing a handful of snow in Orson's face.

Orson spluttered and opened his eyes, bleary from the effects of the tranquiliser. 'Hey, where am I?' he said, confused.

Baron Marackai took a key from his pocket and inserted it into a motor at the end of the machine. The jam press began chugging, large metal cogs slowly turning at its end. As the cogs turned, the two metal slabs sandwiching Orson began to squeeze together.

'Hey, let me out!' the giant said, trying to push the slabs apart.

The Baron chuckled. 'Ha! It's no use struggling, Mr Orson. This jam press is designed to squash any beast, even a big oaf like you.' He licked his lips and smiled. 'Giant jam coming up!'

Baron Marackai moved across to Tiana, trapped inside the glass jar on the machine with wires and dials. He picked up the jar and shook it. 'Wakey, wakey, fairy. Rise and die.'

Tiana tumbled in the jar, among wires that were poking in from the machine. 'Ouch! Hey, what's going on?' she said, waking woozily from being knocked unconscious.

The Baron placed the jar back and flicked a switch on the machine's side. The wires in the jar sparked with electricity.

'*Ow! Eeek!*' Tiana cried, shooting out a burst of sparkles.

Baron Marackai peered in at the fairy. 'It's a sparkle extractor, courtesy of Mr Benzene the pharmacist,' he said, grinning. 'You'll soon be just a dead husk and your sparkles will be all mine! Didn't you know fairy sparkles are worth a fortune?'

'Let her go, Marackai!' Ulf called. 'She doesn't deserve to die!'

'Oh, yes she does. She's a beast! *All beasts deserve to die!*'

Baron Marackai stepped through the falling snow towards Druce. 'Oh, how I hate gargoyles,' he spat, rubbing the stump on his hand where his little finger was missing. He yanked a rope attached to the cement mixer which hung above the gargoyle, and the mixer tilted, pouring wet cement over Druce.

'Blurgh!' Druce gurgled, waking up startled. He tried to jump up, but his hands and feet were chained to pegs in the ground.

'Prepare to be set forever in stone, gargoyle, then sold as an ornament!'

Druce tried to lick the cement from his face with his long yellow tongue, but it was thick and gloopy, and already beginning to harden. 'Blu—'

'I'll tear you to pieces, Baron!' Ulf yelled.

The Baron grinned. 'I doubt that. Ah, here come the last of our little party.'

Blud and Bone came driving towards them in the RSPCB truck. They parked up, and Bone got out and dragged the unconscious Dr Fielding and Professor Farraway from the back, each bound with rope.

'Splendid,' the Baron said. 'Now bury them.'

Bone dumped them in two shallow pits dug in the ground. The falling snow began to settle on them as he went back to the truck. He lifted out two headstones, then stood them at the head of each pit.

One read:

DR FIELDING
GOOD RIDDANCE

And the other:

DADDY
HA HA HA HAAA!

The Baron knelt down and pulled one of the Professor's nose hairs, then he poked Dr Fielding in the eye. 'Wakey wakey!' he called.

Professor Farraway and Dr Fielding's eyes opened woozily. They spluttered, trying to shake the snow from their faces, but it was settling fast.

'Where are we?' Dr Fielding said, disoriented.

'In your graves, being slowly buried under freezing snow!' the Baron replied. He laughed. 'HA HA HAAAA HA HAAAAAA HAAA HA! I WIN! THE RSPCB IS OFFICIALLY OVER!' He glanced up at Ulf, grinning. 'How does it feel to watch your friends die, werewolf?'

Ulf kicked the bars in frustration.

'Why don't you try to save them? There's a bottle of moonjuice above you. In case you wish to transform.'

Ulf looked up, perplexed as to why the Baron would want him to try to save them. But there, dangling on a cord at the top of his cage, was indeed a small bottle of silver liquid – moonjuice from Dr Fielding's laboratory.

The Baron took another key from his pocket and stepped to the machine below Ulf's cage. Ulf felt a shudder and heard a whirring sound as the machine switched on.

'Don't drink it, Ulf!' Professor Farraway called from his snowy grave. 'It must be a trap!'

The Baron kicked snow over the Professor's face to shut him up. 'Oh, don't be a spoilsport, Daddy,' he said. 'Come along, Blud and Bone. We've got beasts to sell.'

'Can't we watch, Sir?' Blud asked. 'I want to see if the werewolf drinks it.'

'Of course he'll drink it, you nincompoop. And we'll be eating wolf burgers for tea! Ha ha ha!'

Still chuckling, the Baron hopped back into the RSPCB Jeep and sped away to find the shopkeepers, followed by Blud and Bone in the truck.

Ulf looked up at the moonjuice

suspiciously, then he glanced down at his friends: Tiana fizzing and popping like a firework inside the sparkle extractor; Orson struggling and groaning in the jam press; Druce setting rigid in the cement; and Professor Farraway and Dr Fielding being slowly buried under falling snow. *I can't just watch my friends die. I have to try and save them.* He reached up and grabbed the bottle of moonjuice. But as he pulled it down he heard a *click* and a trapdoor opened in the floor of his cage. Suddenly he slid down a chute into a solid metal chamber. A huge piston pressed against his back, pushing him slowly forwards towards spinning metal blades at the chamber's end. He was in some kind of beast mincer! *Uh-oh*, he thought, and he glugged the moonjuice to transform.

As it tipped down his throat, Ulf's eyes flashed silver. His spine started bending as his skeleton realigned from biped to quadruped. Muscles bulged all over his body, ripping his T-shirt and jeans, and thick black hair

CHAPTER SEVENTEEN

Inside the jar of the sparkle extractor, Tiana banged on the glass, sparkles fizzing from her. 'Ulf! Don't die!' she called. She could hear his howls from inside the mincing machine, sharp metal blades spinning menacingly at its end.

The fairy was panicking, the electric wires around her zapping her all over. *I have to help Ulf, but who can help me?* she thought. She glanced at Professor Farraway and Dr Fielding in their snowy graves and Orson in the jam press, then over at Druce. *Druce! Of course!* she thought. Tiana had an idea. 'Drucey! Drucey! Look at me!' she called.

The gargoyle's eyes turned, his head unable to move in the setting cement.

The fairy waved and pulled a face. 'One last game, Druce? See if you can get me.'

'Drucey like games,' Druce gurgled, only just able to speak. His long yellow tongue uncoiled from his mouth as he prepared to flick it at the fairy.

'Go on, Druce. Try to get me!'

'Blurgh!' Druce's tongue flicked towards the fairy in the jar. He was trying to play his favourite game – soaking Tiana in spit. The tip of his tongue slapped against the glass.

'That's it, Druce, and again.'

Druce's tongue flicked again, slapping the glass harder this time, and the jar tilted.

'And again, Druce!'

Druce flicked his tongue a third time and the jar toppled and fell, dangling on a wire. 'Well done, Drucey! I knew you could do it!'

Tiana began rocking the jar from side to side, making it swing. She heard Ulf howl

again. *I won't let you die, Ulf!* she thought determinedly.

She rocked harder, swinging the jar against a metal bolt on the machine, and the glass jar cracked. She swung it again and the jar broke open and she flew out. Tiana was free!

The little fairy zoomed to the mincing machine where Ulf was trapped inside. She couldn't fly in or the spinning metal blades would shred her to pieces. Instead she hovered at its end, peering through the blur of blades.

She could just make out Ulf inside, pushing hard against a metal piston, his tail centimetres away from being minced.

Tiana flew to the side of the machine and saw an ignition switch turned to ON, but the Baron had taken its key. 'Ulf, hold on! I'll get help!' she called.

'Blurgh!' Druce gurgled. 'Me help!'

'In a second, Druce, hold on!'

Tiana flew to the snowy graves where the Professor and Dr Fielding were buried. She shot out hot sparkles to melt her way down to the ropes that bound them. She blasted the ropes, burning them through. Dr Fielding and the Professor shook them off and scraped the snow from their faces as they sat up.

'Th-th-thank you, Tiana,' Dr Fielding said, shivering from the cold.

'Quick, you must help Ulf!' Tiana cried. 'He's going to be chopped to pieces in the mincer!'

'We need Orson,' the Professor said, untying his ankles. 'Perhaps he can smash the machine.'

Druce gurgled again from the cement. 'Bluurgh! What about me?'

'In a second, Druce, hold on!' Tiana called.

Professor Farraway and Dr Fielding hurried to Orson. They tried to turn the jam press off but the Baron had taken that key too. Together they pushed, trying to lift the large metal slab that was pressing down on the giant, but it wouldn't budge.

From the mincing machine came another howl.

'Hurry!' Tiana cried.

'Bluurgh!' Druce called again. 'Me me meeee!'

'OK, Druce, I'm coming!' Tiana said. She flew to Druce and blasted the chains around his wrists and ankles. The gargoyle stretched his legs and shook his arms, and great clods of cement fell to the ground. 'Drucey save Fur Face!' he gurgled.

He bounded to the metal mincing machine and reached his hand towards the whirring blades at its end.

'Druce, are you crazy?' Tiana called, flying after him.

But Druce just smiled and turned his fist to stone. He slammed it into the spinning blades and they stopped suddenly with a loud clang.

The Professor and Dr Fielding glanced over. 'Druce?'

The gargoyle's stone fist had jammed the

mincer! Druce pulled it back out from the mangled blades and smiled. 'Fur face okay?' he gurgled.

From inside Ulf ripped the mangled mincing blades apart then burst out alive. 'Thanks, Druce,' he growled, smiling with his werewolf fangs.

'Fur Face free!' Druce gurgled happily.

Ulf bounded to the jam press where Dr Fielding and the Professor were still trying to help Orson. He gripped the metal slab and pushed with all his wolf strength. With Ulf to help too, the slab finally lifted.

Orson gasped, his lungs filling again with air. He slid out sideways then sat on the snow rubbing his squashed nose. 'I thought I was a goner then,' he said. 'Thanks everyone.'

Ulf looked across the paddock seeing shopkeepers pulling tranquilised beasts from their enclosures and loading them on to vehicles. He saw the metamorphs tied in a line to the paddock fence and the Baron over by the freshwater lake where Tony Malone the furniture seller was trying to drag out the tranquilised impossipus.

'It's time to break up this sale,' he growled, and he bounded away across the snow.

CHAPTER EIGHTEEN

At the paddock fence, Jeremy Spoon the café owner was prodding Fred the froglanoid, who was unconscious from the effects of the tranquiliser. The café owner was about to buy Fred for beast goods when he heard Ulf racing towards him. 'What the—'

'Hands off,' Ulf growled, grabbing hold of Mr Spoon.

'Watch out! There's a werewoooooooolf!' the café owner cried as Ulf flung him high in the air over the paddock fence.

The shopkeepers across the beast park turned and stared in horror.

Baron Marackai ran along the edge of the

freshwater lake to the RSPCB Jeep. 'Werewolf, you're supposed to be mince meat!' he yelled.

Ulf slashed through the ropes that bound Freddie the froglanoid. 'Be free!' he growled, shaking him, trying to wake him from the effects of the tranquiliser.

Freddie's eyes opened. 'What's happening, Ulf?' he asked.

'It's time to fight,' Ulf replied.

'Stop the werewolf!' Baron Marackai yelled through his megaphone. 'He's trying to free the metamorphs!'

All around the beast park, the shopkeepers began speeding towards Ulf through the falling snow. They were waving pitchforks and beast prodders from the windows of their vehicles.

Professor Farraway and Dr Fielding ran to Ulf's side.

'Ready for action, Ulf?' the Professor asked.

'Untie the metamorphs,' Ulf told them. 'While I deal with the shopkeepers.'

Orson stepped to Ulf's side. 'Need a little help from a giant, Ulf?' he asked.

'And a fairy!' Tiana added, whizzing over.

'And a gargooool!' Druce gurgled, bounding across the snow.

Ulf smiled, glad to have his friends at his side. 'Let's fight!'

The first shopkeeper to arrive was the butcher Sam Enema. He leapt from his meat van and faced Ulf wielding two large meat cleavers, spinning them like a ninja.

'You're no match for a werewolf,' Ulf growled, and with lightning speed he punched the butcher on the nose. The butcher's eyes crossed, the cleavers dropping from his hands, and he fell backwards into the snow unconscious.

Ulf saw Wanda Wiggins racing over in her pick-up truck. He leapt on to the wig seller's bonnet and smashed his paw through the truck's windscreen, pulling her out and throwing her to the ground.

Wanda Wiggins' wig flew off her head and

underneath she was completely bald. 'My hair!' she cried, covering her head with her hands.

Ulf heard an engine roar and looked round, seeing Alfred Jacobs the jam maker accelerating across the snow in his jam van. 'I'll run you down and smear you on toast!' he yelled from his window.

'This one's mine,' Orson said. The giant stomped forwards and brought his huge boot crashing down on the jam-maker's van, squashing it flat. He reached in through the van's window and plucked the jam maker out.

'Ahhh! Get off me!' Alfred Jacobs cried.

'How do *you* like being squashed?' Orson said, squeezing the jam maker in his big hand, then hurling him across the park.

Jemima Fatchuck's pie truck skidded to a halt beside Ulf, and the pie maker got out brandishing a rolling pin. 'I'll have you in my pie!' she cried.

Ulf leapt and bit her rolling pin in two. 'Oh no you won't,' he growled. He bundled her to the ground, rolling her over and over in the snow turning her into a human snowball, just her pudgy head and feet sticking out. Then he bowled her across the paddock.

'Heeeeeeeelp!' she cried, smashing into more of the shopkeepers, toppling them like skittles.

Ulf glanced round to see Tiana shoot across the paddock and dive in the window of Arnold Benzene's medicines van, blasting her sparkles at the pharmacist.

'Ouch! Ow! I can't see where I'm going!' the pharmacist cried, skidding straight into the freshwater lake.

Tiana flew back to Ulf. 'That's what I think of his nasty sparkle extractor machine.'

Baron Marackai's voice blared out through his megaphone: 'Stop dithering and fight!'

Tony Malone the furniture seller jumped down from the cab of his lorry wielding a pitchfork. He jabbed it at Ulf. 'I'll make cushion covers with your fur!' he said.

Druce leapt to Ulf's side and flicked his tongue out, snatching the pitchfork from

Tony Malone's hand. 'Fur Face not for cushions!' he gurgled, bashing the furniture seller with his stone fist.

'Thanks Druce,' Ulf said, racing to the back of the lorry. He ripped open the lorry doors and saw two groggy trolls inside. 'Come on, out you come,' he said to them.

But as he was helping the trolls, he heard Baron Marackai calling through his megaphone: 'What's the matter with you lot? Blud, Bone, see to the werewolf.'

Ulf heard wheels skidding on the snow behind him and span round.

Blud and Bone jumped from the RSPCB truck pointing electric beast prodders.

'Want some of this, werewolf?' Bone said, jabbing one towards Ulf.

Ulf leapt to the side, dodging the prodder.

'Or this!' Blud said, swiping at him with his prodder. Ulf leapt back, dodging it too, but then Bone came at him from behind, zapping Ulf in the back.

Ulf felt an electric current shoot through

him and he fell to the ground, stunned.

'Ha! Zap the mangy flea bag again!' Blud called.

Bone raised the prodder over Ulf, about to strike.

'I wouldn't do that if I were you,' a voice boomed.

It was Orson, striding over to help. The giant leant down and lifted Bone into the air. 'Think you're a big man, do you? Well, you're not as big as me!'

He threw Bone high into the air and the Baron's henchman landed with a thud in the back of the RSPCB truck.

Ulf got to his feet and faced Blud. 'Who did you say was a mangy flea bag?' he asked.

'Um... er...' Blud turned to run but Ulf grabbed him and hurled him into the back of the truck with Bone.

The two men hugged one another, whimpering fearfully in the falling snow, 'Please don't hurt us!'

'Nice team work, Ulf,' Orson said, taking a

rope from the truck and tying the Baron's henchmen up.

'You imbeciles!' Baron Marackai yelled from his Jeep, furious at how events were turning out.

Ulf looked around the beast park. The RSPCB were winning. Even the metamorphs were joining in the fight now, transforming into their beast forms as each was freed by Dr Fielding and the Professor.

Al grew his mighty wings and flew into the air, then swooped down on Mary Deacon, plucking the dress shop owner from the ground with his talons.

'Help! Put me down!' she cried.

Zena the werecat transformed and pounced on Jemima De Laig, pinning the jeweller to the ground with her cat claws.

Fred the froglanoid hopped through the air and landed on top of Jeremy Spoon the café owner, sending him sprawling in the snow. 'Frogs' legs soup is off the menu!' he said.

Across the beast park some of the beasts

were waking from their tranquilised states and fighting back too. Up on Troll Crag, Ulf spotted a veil lizard, bright red with anger, whacking Bettina Scrag's truck with its tail.

Down at the freshwater lake, Tomiko the impossipus was now whipping out her tentacles and grabbing any shopkeepers that came too close.

Ulf looked for Baron Marackai and saw him driving around the edge of the paddock in the RSPCB Jeep, trying to steer clear of the fight. The beast hunter sped through the paddock gates towards the yard. Ulf realised he was heading for the main gates. 'Orson, stop Marackai! He's trying to escape!' he called.

In three giant strides, Orson leapt over the paddock fence, over the fire-zone into the yard, then into the forecourt, blocking the Baron's escape. 'Oh, no you don't, Marackai!' he boomed.

Baron Marackai swerved, narrowly avoiding the giant's boot.

'It's over, Marackai. There's no escape!' Orson said.

'Wanna bet?' the Baron yelled back. 'Just you watch me!' He did a U-turn, spinning the Jeep around, and sped back through the paddock in the direction of the Dark Forest.

The Professor came skidding to Ulf's side on a quad bike. 'We'll catch him, Ulf!'

'You take the marsh track, Professor, and try to cut him off!' Ulf growled.

'Good thinking,' the Professor replied. 'He'll have nowhere to go.'

'**Whatever it takes, we won't let him get away this time**,' Ulf said, and he set off in pursuit of the Baron.

CHAPTER NINETEEN

Ulf bounded on all fours into the Dark Forest, sprinting along a track through the trees as he chased after Baron Marackai.

'You'll never catch me!' the Baron called, racing away in the RSPCB truck. He skidded around corners and bumped over the snow.

Ulf ran after him, leaping over fallen logs and bursting through snowdrifts.

As the Baron sped out of the Dark Forest and on to the bridge over the meat-eaters' enclosures, Ulf roared, 'Stop right there, Baron!'

Baron Marackai glanced back and aimed a pistol at him. *BANG!* Ulf ducked and the bullet went whizzing over his head.

'Need any help, Ulf?' he heard. It was Tiana, flying rapidly after him.

'I'm going to tear him to pieces, Tiana,' Ulf growled.

The Baron sped up across the Great Grazing Grounds, swerving to avoid the lumbering beasts, and Ulf and Tiana raced after him.

As Ulf ran across the snowy uplands towards Sunset Mountain, he spotted Professor Farraway zooming round from the marsh track on his quad bike. They had the Baron trapped in a pincer movement! 'Marackai can't get away now,' he called to Tiana.

But as he raced towards the mountain, the Baron veered left, heading towards the seawater lagoon. He went speeding along its dockside. He was laughing.

Suddenly Ulf noticed the RSPCB submersible tied up at the lagoon's edge. The Baron was speeding towards it! 'He's trying to escape out to sea, Tiana!' Ulf yelled.

Thinking quickly, Ulf leapt off the track into the freezing lagoon. He swam as fast as he could, using his wolf strength to power through the icy water, and scrambled on to the submersible just as the Baron skidded to a halt on the dockside.

'Out of my way, werewolf!' the Baron said, pointing his gun at Ulf again.

'The game's up, Marackai!' Ulf growled. 'There's no way out!'

The Baron had his finger on the trigger and was about to pull it as Tiana zoomed down, blasting him with her sparkles. The gun went off and the bullet went whizzing past Ulf's ear, sparking on the submersible's metal hull.

'Curses!' the Baron yelled. He put the Jeep into reverse and slammed his foot on the accelerator, reversing back along the dockside. 'You'll never stop me!'

But the Baron wasn't looking where he was going. He didn't see Professor Farraway speeding to the dockside on his quad bike.

'Watch out!' Ulf cried.

Baron Marackai turned, seeing his father just as the Jeep and the quad bike collided, hurling the

Professor from his seat across the snow and ice.

'Professor, are you okay?' Ulf called, bounding towards him.

But Baron Marackai was closer. He jumped from the dented Jeep and grabbed Professor Farraway, pointing the gun at his head. 'Stay back, werewolf, or Daddy dies!'

The Baron dragged the Professor semi-conscious towards the foot of Sunset Mountain. He began climbing up the mountain, heaving the Professor after him. He fired at Ulf to keep him back. Ulf ducked and the bullet thudded into the snow.

'Give up, Marackai,' Ulf called, as the Baron climbed higher, edging round the mountainside out of sight.

'Never!' came the reply.

Ulf and Tiana continued in hot pursuit, trying not to be seen. Higher and higher they climbed after the Baron, the snow falling in blinding flurries, a freezing mist thickening around them.

Ulf climbed on to a large plateau at the very

top of the mountain and saw Marackai facing him, his pistol still pointed at the Professor. Professor Farraway could hardly stand and his nose was bleeding.

'Let the Professor go, Marackai,' Ulf growled.

The Baron smiled. 'No can do, werewolf. Fairy, fly off and tell Dr Fielding I want the RSPCB helicopter up here immediately for my escape. And no funny business.'

'No way! I'm not helping you escape,' Tiana said.

'Oh yes you are! Or look what happens.' Without warning, the Baron pointed his pistol at Ulf and fired.

Ulf felt a stinging pain in his arm. He looked down and saw blood running where he had been shot.

'No!' Tiana shrieked.

CHAPTER TWENTY

Tiana zoomed to Ulf's side. 'Are you okay, Ulf?'

'I'll live,' Ulf said, clutching his wounded arm.

'I said I want that helicopter. Now!' Baron Marackai ordered. 'Go fairy. Or I'll shoot again!'

'Okay, okay! I'm going,' Tiana cried. 'Please don't hurt anyone!' And she darted off through the mist and snow to find Dr Fielding.

'And now you can go too, werewolf,' the Baron said. 'Or the Professor dies!'

'Ulf, don't listen to him,' Professor Farraway said weakly. 'I've been a ghost before. I can be one again.'

Ulf snarled at the Baron, trying to ignore the pain in his arm. Then he took a step back down the mountainside, not wanting to endanger the Professor.

'Not that way,' the Baron said to him. 'Take the quick way down, over that ledge to your left.'

He pointed the gun at Ulf, directing him to a ledge at the side of the mountain top. It was a sheer drop down through the snowy mists.

'No, Ulf, you'll die!' Professor Farraway called.

Baron Marackai smiled. 'Jump, werewolf. You have five seconds, or I'll shoot the Professor, and then *you*. Five… four…'

From the mists below Ulf heard a sound: '*Twit Twoo Twit Twoo!*'

He glanced back to Marackai.

'… two… one…'

Marackai cocked the trigger on his pistol, and Ulf leapt from the mountain. Down he fell through the mist. He heard the beating of wings and briefly saw Al swooping up towards him. He landed on Al's feathery back. 'Thanks,' Ulf said.

'Good of you to drop by,' the owl-man replied, smiling.

'We have to get Marackai, Al!' Ulf whispered. He could hear the Baron's laughter from above. 'Ha ha ha! That werewolf was more stupid than I thought!'

Al circled the mountain then soared high above it.

'That werewolf is worth ten of you,' Ulf heard the Professor reply.

Al dived towards the sound, gliding silently through the snowy air.

Ulf saw Baron Marackai pointing his gun at the Professor. 'Now, Al,' he whispered.

Al reached out his talons and grabbed hold of the Baron from above, lifting him away.

Ulf kicked the pistol from the Baron's hand.

'Wha—' Baron Marackai exclaimed in surprise. He struggled and screamed, trying to wriggle free. 'Let me go, you overgrown barn owl!'

But Al had him firmly in his grasp. The owl-man glided through the falling snow back over the Dark Forest, then swooped down over the freshwater lake and the paddock where the shopkeepers had been rounded up, and metamorphs were tying them up with ropes.

'The sale's over, Marackai,' Ulf said as they flew above Farraway Hall where Tiana and Dr Fielding were hurrying to the helicopter in the forecourt. 'We got him!' Ulf called down.

Tiana and Dr Fielding looked up. 'Well done, Ulf!'

'What shall we do with him?' Al asked, circling above the yard.

Below, Ulf saw Orson leading Rumbold the slurper back to the big beast barn.

Ulf had an idea. 'Marackai, let's see how Rumbold likes the taste of you,' he said.

'Nooooo!' the Baron shrieked.

Al let go of the Baron, dropping him directly above the slurper. 'Orson, it's feeding time for Rumbold!'

The giant and the slurper looked up.

Rumbold opened his huge slobbering mouth.

'I HATE YOU, WEREWOOOOOOOOLF!' the Baron cried, dropping out of sight down Rumbold's slimy throat.

Rumbold the slurper belched. They'd done it! Marackai was trapped and the RSPCB was saved! Ulf licked his fangs, smiling, then threw his head back and howled.

CHAPTER TWENTY-ONE

Later that afternoon, when the effects of the moonjuice had worn off, Ulf returned to his boy self.

Tiana flew to find him, hovering in the doorway to his den. 'You were wild!' she said, smiling.

'Was I?' Ulf asked her, pulling on a fresh T-shirt and jeans that Dr Fielding had laid ready for him. He couldn't remember much. It was all a bit of a blur.

'You were amazing, Ulf. You transformed and saved us, and the metamorphs.'

Ulf remembered drinking the moonjuice and transforming in the mincing machine.

'I'd have been mincemeat if it wasn't for you, Tiana,' he replied. 'You and Druce saved *my* life.'

Tiana blushed. 'Any time, Ulf,' she said. 'Come on, come and say goodbye. The metamorphs are about to leave.'

She fluttered off, and Ulf followed her, up the side of the paddock to Farraway Hall. He saw the wrecked beast machines, and tyre tracks criss-crossing in the snow. 'What happened to all the shopkeepers?' he asked.

'Oh, after your moonjuice wore off, NICE arrived. They're taking the shopkeepers away to prison. Blud and Bone too.'

'And what about Marackai?'

Tiana giggled. 'He still hasn't passed through Rumbold yet.'

In the yard outside the house, agents from NICE were standing with Orson at the doors of the big beast barn waiting for Marackai to come out from the slurper's bottom.

Orson gave a thumb's-up, seeing Ulf. 'You trapped him good and proper, Ulf. He's going to stink something rotten when he appears.'

Ulf smiled. 'And then he's going straight to prison, Orson. For good.'

Ulf saw a prison van parked in the forecourt with the shopkeepers and Blud and Bone peering out through the van's barred window.

He saw Professor Farraway and Dr Fielding talking to Al nearby, and the other metamorphs waiting by the shopkeepers' vans and trucks. Everyone cheered as Ulf approached.

'You saved us all, Ulf,' Dr Fielding said. 'The metamorphs *and* the RSPCB.'

She rushed over and gave him a hug.

Ulf could feel his face going red. 'I was just being a werewolf,' he replied.

Al reached down and shook Ulf's hand. 'Your parents would be proud of you,' he said.

'Will you be safe back in the city now, Al?' Ulf asked. 'What about the public?'

'We'll be fine, Ulf, thanks to you. Dolores

Larkin has kindly agreed to write an article in tomorrow's *City Gazette* telling the public the truth about beasts.'

'Dolores Larkin?' Ulf asked, confused. 'But Dolores Larkin was Marack—'

'We found the real Miss Larkin locked in the boot of her little blue car,' Professor Farraway said. 'Marackai had stolen that car from her and tied her up in there when he'd put on his disguise.'

A short woman with round-rimmed glasses peered from behind the Professor with a notebook and pen in her hand. 'I've heard all about you, Ulf. What a story! I'll be sure to tell everyone how brave you were.'

Ulf blushed bashfully.

Big Al leaned down to him. 'It's been a pleasure to meet you, Ulf. Come and visit us in the city any time. Who knows, you might even want to come and live with us one day.'

'Maybe,' Ulf replied. 'I'd like that.'

The metamorphs got into the shopkeepers' vehicles, with Big Al, Fred the froglanoid,

Zena the werecat and Charna the spidrax driving. Ulf waved goodbye as the vans and trucks filed through the main gates and away up the drive.

At that moment there came an almighty rumble from the big beast barn, followed by a shrill cry. 'Eyugh!'

Ulf turned back and saw three NICE agents in contamination suits and gas masks dragging a dishevelled figure in handcuffs away from the big beast barn. It was Baron Marackai, covered from head to toe in stinky brown slime.

'You bunch of do-gooders!' the Baron cried.

Ulf watched as the NICE agents bundled the beast hunter into the waiting prison van. 'You're going to prison, Marackai,' Ulf called.

'I'll have my revenge yet,' the Baron replied. 'You'll see, I'll be baaaa—!'

A NICE agent slammed the door of the prison van shut, and Ulf smiled as it drove away out of the forecourt and up the driveway, with Marackai scowling from its barred window. This time the beast hunter was gone for good.

As the Baron was driven away, Druce the gargoyle blew a raspberry from the rooftop of Farraway Hall. He started singing. 'He comes in the night with his knife and his gun. Marackai stinks now! Fur Face won!'

Ulf felt Dr Fielding's hand on his shoulder. 'I've got something for you, Ulf,' she said. 'Everyone, over here, please.'

Orson, Tiana and Professor Farraway came over, and Druce hopped on to the front porch.

'What is it?' Ulf asked.

Dr Fielding reached into her lab coat pocket and took out a brand new RSPCB agent's badge. She pinned it to Ulf's T-shirt. 'Congratulations, Ulf. In recent months you have excelled in protecting all kinds of beasts: dragons, sea monsters, trolls, vampires, zombies, ghosts and even metamorphs. I hereby proclaim you an official RSPCB agent.'

Ulf looked from the badge to his friends, all smiling at him.

'Well done Ulf,' Professor Farraway said.

'You deserve it, Ulf,' Orson told him, ruffling Ulf's hair with his finger.

Tiana perched on his badge. 'You won't go and live in the city just yet though, will you, Ulf? We are still best friends, aren't we?'

'Don't worry, Tiana. I like it here too much to go anywhere just yet.'

'Right then, we'd better all get back to work,' Dr Fielding said. 'This place needs a good clean up.'

'As long as I don't have to go near that slurper,' Tiana said. 'Rumbold stinks!'

'Ulf, why don't you and I do the evening rounds together, and check on the beasts?' Professor Farraway said. 'I seem to recall I promised to show you how to hatch griffins' eggs. How about it?'

'You bet!' Ulf said.

They headed to the Kit Room and fetched a wheelbarrow and a couple of shovels.

'Now, Ulf, did I ever tell you about the time I rescued a griffin nest from poachers?' Professor Farraway asked.

'No, Professor, I don't think you did.'

'Well, I was in the Indian jungle when I came upon this most peculiar nest the size of a trampoline…'

Ulf smiled and, as the afternoon sun shone over the snowy rescue centre, he and the Professor headed off side-by-side into the beast park.

THE END

978 1 84738 837 7 £5.99 PB

Can Ulf defeat the beast hunter?

The first thrilling adventure in the Beastly Business series.

SIMON AND SCHUSTER
A CBS Company

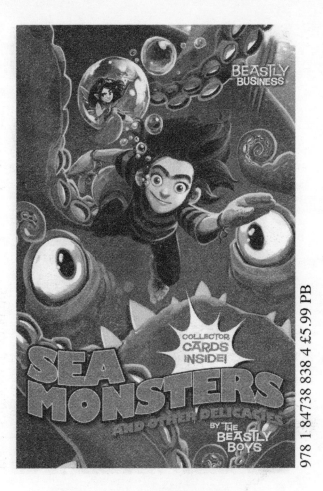

Get ready for the Beast Feast!

The second exciting adventure in the Beastly Business series.

SIMON AND SCHUSTER
A CBS Company

COLLECTOR CARDS INSIDE!

BANG GOES A TROLL

BY THE BEASTLY BOYS

BEASTLY BUSINESS

978 0 85707 181 1 £5.99 PB

It's time to hunt the hunters!

The third fantastic adventure in the Beastly Business series.

SIMON AND SCHUSTER
A CBS Company

COLLECTOR CARDS INSIDE!

THE JUNGLE VAMPIRE

BY THE BEASTLY BOYS

978 0 85707 192 7 £5.99 PB

Beware the vampire's bite!

The fourth fearsome adventure in the Beastly Business series.

SIMON AND SCHUSTER
A CBS Company

Can Ulf defeat the undead?

The fifth gripping adventure in the Beastly Business series.

SIMON AND SCHUSTER
A CBS Company

BEASTLY
BUSINESS

**The Beastly Boys
are David Sinden,
Matthew Morgan and
Guy Macdonald.** They met at
school in Kent, and have been
friends ever since.

SIMON AND SCHUSTER
A CBS Company

Visit www.beastlybusiness.com for lots of exciting extras - meet the authors, join the RSPCB and discover the secrets of the beasts ...!